The Monkey and The Tiger

Two Chinese Detective Stories by

ROBERT VAN GULIK

*With eight illustrations
drawn by the author in Chinese style*

The University of Chicago Press

This edition is reprinted by arrangement with Charles
Scribner's Sons, an imprint of Macmillan Publishing
Company.

The University of Chicago Press, Chicago 60637
Copyright © 1965 Robert H. van Gulik
All rights reserved. Published 1965
University of Chicago Press edition 1992
Printed in the United States of America
99 98 97 96 95 94   6 5 4 3 2

ISBN 0-226-84869-8 (pbk.)

Library of Congress Cataloging-in-Publication Data

Gulik, Robert Hans van, 1910–1967.
    The monkey and the tiger : two Chinese detective
stories / by Robert van Gulik.—University of Chicago
Press ed.
      p.   cm.—(Phoenix fiction)
      1. Ti, Jên-chieh, 629–700—Fiction.   2. China—
History—T'ang dynasty, 618–907—Fiction.   3. Detective
and mystery stories, English.   I. Title.   II. Series.
PR9130.9.G8M66   1992
823—dc20   92-22578
                                                           CIP

⊗ The paper used in this publication meets the minimum
requirements of the American National Standard for
Information Sciences—Permanence of Paper for Printed
Library Materials, ANSI Z39.48-1984

The Monkey and The Tiger

DRAMATIS PERSONAE

Note that in Chinese the surname—here printed
in capitals—precedes the personal name

The Morning of the Monkey:

Judge DEE	magistrate of Han-yuan, in A.D. 666
TAO Gan	one of his lieutenants
WANG	a pharmacist
LENG	a pawnbroker
SENG Kiu	a vagabond
Miss SENG	his sister
CHANG	another vagabond

The Night of the Tiger:

Judge DEE	travelling from Pei-chow to the capital, in A.D. 676.
MIN Liang	a wealthy landowner
MIN Kee-yü	his daughter
Mr MIN	his younger brother, a tea merchant.
YEN Yuan	bailiff of the Min estate
LIAO	the steward
Aster	a maidservant

In the accompanying Chinese zodiac—always represented with the south at the top—the images of the Monkey and the Tiger indicate their correct position; the other animals are represented by their cyclical signs only. The complete set, known as the 'Twelve Branches of Heaven', consists of 1 Rat (Aries), 2 Cow (Taurus), 3 Tiger (Gemini), 4 Hare (Cancer), 5 Dragon (Leo), 6 Serpent (Virgo), 7 Horse (Libra), 8 Sheep (Scorpio), 9 Monkey (Sagittarius), 10 Cock (Capricorn), 11 Dog (Aquarius) and 12 Pig (Pisces). This series also indicates the 24 hours of a natural day: the Rat 11-1 a.m., the Cow 1-3 a.m., etc.

A second cyclical series (not depicted here) consists of the 'Ten Stems of Earth', which represents also the Five Elements and the Five Planets, viz. I *chia*, II *yi* (both wood and Jupiter), III *ping*, IV *ting* (*fire* and Mars), V *mou*, VI *chi* (*earth* and Saturn), VII *keng*, VIII *hsin* (*metal* and Venus), IX *Jen*, X *kuei* (*water* and Mercury). The twelve 'branches', combined with the ten 'stems', form a sexagenary cycle: I-1, II-2, III-3, IV-4, V-5, VI-6, VII-7, VIII-8, IX-9, X-10, I-11, II-12, III-1, IV-2 and so on till X-12. This cycle of sixty double signs is the basis of Chinese chronology. Six cycles indicate the 360 days of a tropical year and 'the twelve lunar months, and also the years themselves in an ever-repeating series of sixty—'A cycle of Cathay'! The year 1900 was VII-1, a year of the Rat, and we are living now in the cycle that began in 1924 with the year of the Rat I-1; this particular cycle ends in 1984. The current year, 1965, is II-6, a year of the Serpent, 1966 will be III-7, a year of the Horse.

The octagonal design in the centre of the zodiac is explained in the Postscript.

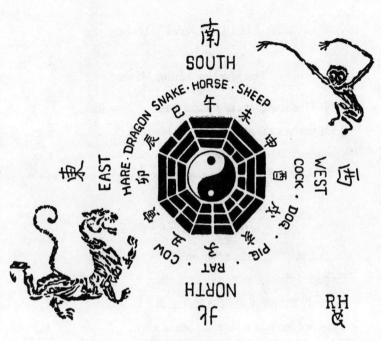

THE CHINESE ZODIAC

ILLUSTRATIONS

The Morning of the Monkey

The Night of the Tiger

A sketchmap of the flooded area appears on page 85

THE MORNING OF THE MONKEY

Dedicated to the memory of my good friend the gibbon Bubu, died at Port Dickson, Malaya, 12 July 1962.

THE MORNING OF THE MONKEY

Judge Dee was enjoying the cool summer morning in the open gallery built along the rear of his official residence. He had just finished breakfast inside with his family, and now was having his tea there all alone, as had become his fixed habit during the year he had been serving as magistrate of the lake district Han-yuan.* He had drawn his rattan armchair close to the carved marble balustrade. Slowly stroking his long black beard, he gazed up contentedly at the tall trees and dense undergrowth covering the mountain slope that rose directly in front of the gallery like a protecting wall of cool verdure. From it came the busy twitter of small birds, and the murmur of the cascade farther along. It was a pity, he thought, that these relaxed moments of peaceful enjoyment were so brief. Presently he would have to go to the chancery in the front section of the tribunal compound, and have a look at the official correspondence that had come in.

Suddenly there was the sound of rustling leaves and breaking twigs. Two furry black shapes came rushing through the tree-tops, swinging from branch to branch by their long, thin arms, and leaving a rain of falling leaves in their wake. The judge looked after the gibbons with a smile. He never tired of admiring their lithe grace as they came speeding past. Shy as they were, the gibbons living on the mountain slope had

* It was here that Judge Dee solved the *Chinese Lake Murders*, London, Michael Joseph, 1960.

become accustomed to that solitary figure sitting there every morning. Sometimes one of them would stop for one brief moment and deftly catch the banana Judge Dee threw at him.

Again the leaves rustled. Now another gibbon came into sight. He moved slowly, using only one long arm and his hand-like feet. He was carrying a small object in his left hand. The gibbon halted in front of the gallery and, perched on a lower branch, darted an inquisitive look at the judge from his round, brown eyes. Now Judge Dee saw what the animal had in his left hand: it was a golden ring with a large, sparkling green stone. He knew that gibbons often snatch small objects that catch their fancy, but also that their interest is short-lived, especially if they find they can't eat what they have picked up. If he couldn't make the gibbon drop the ring then and there, he would throw it away somewhere in the forest, and the owner would never recover it.

Since the judge had no fruit at hand to distract the gibbon's attention from the ring, he quickly took his tinderbox from his sleeve and began to arrange its contents on the tea-table, carefully examining and sniffing at each object. He saw out of the corner of his eye that the gibbon was watching him. Soon he let the ring drop, swung himself down to the lowest branch and remained hanging there by his long, spidery arms, following Judge Dee's every gesture with eager interest. The judge noticed that a few blades of straw were sticking to the gibbon's black fur. He couldn't hold the fickle animal's attention for long. The gibbon called out a friendly 'Wak wak!' then swung itself up onto a higher branch, and disappeared among the green leaves.

Judge Dee stepped over the balustrade and down onto the moss-covered boulders that lined the foot of the mountain slope. Soon he had spotted the glittering ring. He picked it

JUDGE DEE SAW THAT THE GIBBON WAS WATCHING HIM

up and climbed back onto the gallery. A closer examination proved that it was rather large, evidently a man's ring. It consisted of two intertwined dragons of solid gold, and the emerald was unusually big and of excellent quality. The owner would be glad to get this valuable antique specimen back. Just when he was about to put the ring away in his sleeve, his eye fell on a few rust-brown spots on its inside. Creasing his bushy eyebrows, he brought the ring closer. The stains looked uncommonly like dried blood.

He turned round and clapped his hands. When his old house steward came shuffling out to the gallery, he asked:

'What houses stand on the mountain slope over there, steward?'

'There are none, sir. The slope is much too steep, and covered entirely by the dense forest. There are several villas on top of the ridge, though.'

'Yes, I remember having seen those summer villas. Do you happen to know who is living there?'

'Well, sir, the pawnbroker Leng, for instance. And also Wang, the pharmacist.'

'Leng I don't know. And Wang, you say? I suppose you mean the owner of the large pharmacy in the market-place, opposite the Temple of Confucius? A small, dapper fellow, always looking rather worried?'

'Yes indeed, sir. He has good reasons to look worried, too, sir. His business isn't going very well this year, I heard. And his only son is mentally defective. He'll be twenty next year, and still he can neither read nor write. I don't know what is to become of a boy like that. . . .'

Judge Dee nodded absent-mindedly. The villas on the ridge were out, for gibbons are too shy to venture into an inhabited area. He could have picked it up, of course, in a quiet corner of a large garden up there. But even then he

6

would have thrown it away long before he had traversed the forest and arrived at the foot of the slope. The gibbon must have found the ring much farther down.

He dismissed the steward and had another look at the ring. The glitter of the emerald seemed to have become dull suddenly, it had become a sombre eye that fixed him with a mournful stare. Annoyed at his discomfiture, he quickly put it back into his sleeve. He would issue a public notice describing the ring, and then the owner would soon present himself at the tribunal and that would be the end of it. He went inside, and walked through his residence to his front garden, and from there on to the large central courtyard of the tribunal compound.

It was fairly cool there, for the big buildings surrounding the yard protected it from the morning sun. The headman of the constables was inspecting the equipment of a dozen of his men, lined up in the centre of the courtyard. All sprang to attention when they saw the magistrate approaching. Judge Dee was about to walk past them, on to the chancery over on the other side, when a sudden thought made him halt in his steps. He asked the headman:

'Do you know of any inhabited place in the forest on the mountain slope, behind my residence?'

'No, Your Honour, there are no houses, as far as I know. Half-way up there is a hut, though. A small log-cabin, formerly used by a woodcutter. It has been standing empty for a long time now.' Then he added importantly: 'Vagabonds often stay there for the night, sir. That's why I go up there regularly. Just to see that they make no mischief.'

This might fit. In a deserted hut, half-way up the slope . . .

'What do you call regularly?' he asked sharply.

'Well, I mean to say . . . once every five or six weeks, sir. I . . .'

7

'I don't call that regularly!' the judge interrupted him curtly. 'I expect you to . . .' He broke off in mid-sentence. This wouldn't do. A vague, uneasy feeling oughtn't to make him lose his temper. It must be the savoury sitting heavily on his stomach that had spoilt his pleasant, relaxed mood. He shouldn't take meat with the morning rice . . . He resumed, in a more friendly manner:

'How far is that hut from here, headman?'

'A quarter of an hour's walk, sir. On the narrow footpath that leads up the slope.'

'Right. Call Tao Gan here!'

The headman ran to the chancery. He came back with a gaunt, elderly man, clad in a long robe of faded brown cotton and with a high square cap of black gauze on his head. He had a long, melancholy face with a drooping moustache and a wispy chinbeard, and three long hairs waxed from the wart on his left cheek. When Tao Gan had wished his chief a good morning, Judge Dee took his assistant to the corner of the yard. He showed him the ring and told him how he had got it. 'You notice the dried blood sticking to it. Probably the owner cut his hand when taking a walk in the forest. He took the ring off before washing his hand in the brook, and then the gibbon snatched it. Since it is quite a valuable piece, and since we have still an hour before the morning session begins, we'll go up there and have a look. Perhaps the owner is still wandering about searching for his ring. Were there any important letters by the morning courier?'

Tao Gan's long, sallow face fell as he replied:

'There was a brief note from Chiang-pei, from our Sergeant Hoong, sir. He reports that Ma Joong and Chiao Tai haven't yet succeeded in discovering a clue.'

Judge Dee frowned. Sergeant Hoong and his two other lieutenants had left for the neighbouring district of Chiang-

8

pei two days before, in order to assist Judge Dee's colleague there who was working on a difficult case with ramifications in his own district. 'Well,' he said with a sigh, 'let's go. A brisk walk will do us good!' He beckoned the headman and told him to accompany them with two constables.

They left the tribunal compound by the back door, and, a little way along the narrow mud road, the headman took a footpath that led up into the forest.

The path rose gradually in a zig-zag pattern but it was still a stiff climb. They met nobody and the only sound they heard was the twittering of the birds, high up in the tree-tops. After about a quarter of an hour the headman halted and pointed at a cluster of tall trees farther up.

'There it is, sir!' he announced.

Soon they found themselves in a small clearing surrounded by high oak trees. In the rear stood a small log-cabin with a mossy thatched roof. The door was closed, the only window shuttered. In front stood a chopping-block made of an old tree trunk; beside it was a heap of straw. It was still as the grave; the place seemed completely deserted.

Judge Dee walked through the tall, wet grass and pulled the door open. In the semi-dark interior he saw a deal table with two footstools, and against the back wall a bare plank-bed. On the floor in front lay the still figure of a man, clad in a jacket and trousers of faded blue cloth. His jaw was sagging, his glazed eyes wide open.

The judge quickly turned round and ordered the headman to open the shutters. Then he and Tao Gan squatted down by the side of the prone figure. It was an elderly man, thin but rather tall. He had a broad, regular face with a grey moustache and a short, neatly-trimmed goatee. The grey hair on top of the head was a mass of clotted blood. The right hand was folded over the breast, the left stretched out, close against the side of the body. Judge Dee tried to lift the arm

9

but found it had stiffened completely. 'Must have died late last night!' he muttered.

'What happened to his left hand, sir?' Tao Gan asked.

Four fingers had been cut off just at the last joint, leaving only blood-covered stumps. Only the thumb was intact.

The judge studied the sunburnt, mutilated hand carefully.

'Do you see that narrow band of white skin round the index, Tao Gan? Its irregular outline corresponds to that of the intertwined dragons of the emerald ring. My hunch was right. This is the owner, and he was murdered.' He got up and told the headman, 'Let your men carry the corpse outside!'

While the two constables were dragging the dead man away, Judge Dee and Tao Gan quickly searched the hut. The floor, the table and the two stools were covered by a thick layer of dust, but the plank-bed had been cleaned very thoroughly. They did not see a single bloodstain. Pointing at the many confused footprints in the dust on the floor, Tao Gan remarked:

'Evidently a number of people were about here last night. This print here would seem to be left by a small, pointed woman's shoe. And that there by a man's shoe, and a very big one too!'

The judge nodded. He studied the floor a while, then said: 'I don't see any traces of the body having been dragged across the floor, so it must have been carried inside. They neatly cleaned the plank-bed. Then, instead of putting the body there, they deposited it on the floor! Strange affair! Well, let's have a second look at the corpse.'

Outside Judge Dee pointed at the heap of straw and resumed:

'Everything fits, Tao Gan. I noticed a few blades of straw clinging to the gibbon's fur. When the body was being carried to the hut, the ring slipped from the stump of the left index and fell into the straw. When the gibbon passed by here early this morning, his sharp eyes spotted the glittering object among the straw, and he picked it up. It took us a quarter of an hour to come here along the winding path, but as the crow flies it's but a short distance from here to the trees at the foot of the slope, behind my house. It took the gibbon very little time to rush down through the tree-tops.'

Tao Gan stooped and examined the chopping-block.

'There are no traces of blood here, sir. And the four cut-off fingers are nowhere to be seen.'

'Evidently the man was mutilated and murdered some-where else,' the judge said. 'His dead body was carried up here afterwards.'

'Then the murderer must have been a hefty fellow, sir. It isn't an easy job to carry a body all the way up here. Unless the murderer had assistance, of course.'

'Search him!'

As Tao Gan began to go through the dead man's clothes, Judge Dee carefully examined the head. He thought that the skull must have been bashed in from behind, with a fairly small but heavy instrument, probably an iron hammer. Then he studied the intact right hand. The palm and the inside of the fingers were rather horny, but the nails were fairly long and well kept.

'There's absolutely nothing, sir!' Tao Gan exclaimed as he righted himself. 'Not even a handkerchief! The murderer must have taken away everything that could have led to the identification of his victim.'

'We do have the ring, however,' the judge observed. 'He had doubtless planned to take that too. When he found it missing, he must have realized that it fell off the mutilated hand somewhere on the way here. He probably searched for

11

it with a lantern, but in vain.' He turned to the headman, who was chewing on a toothpick with a bored look, and asked curtly: 'Ever seen this man before?'

The headman sprang to attention.

'No, Your Honour. Never!' He cast a questioning look at the two constables. When they shook their heads, he added: 'Must be a vagabond from up-country, sir.'

'Tell your men to make a stretcher from a couple of thick branches and take the body to the tribunal. Let the clerks and the rest of the court personnel file past it, and see whether any of them knows the man. After you have warned the coroner, go to Mr Wang's pharmacy in the market-place, and ask him to come and see me in my office.'

While walking downhill Tao Gan asked curiously:

'Do you think that pharmacist knows more about this, sir?'

'Oh no. But it had just occurred to me that the dead body might as well have been carried down as up hill! Therefore I want to ask Wang whether there was a fight among vagabonds or other riff-raff on the ridge last night. At the same time I want to ask him who else is living there, beside himself and that pawnbroker Leng. Heaven, my robe is caught!'

As Tao Gan was prying loose the thorny branch, Judge Dee went on: 'The dead man's dress points to a labourer or an artisan, but he has the face of an intellectual. And his sunburnt and calloused but well-kept hand suggests an educated man of means, who likes to live outdoors. I conclude that he was a man of means from the fact that he possessed that expensive emerald ring.'

Tao Gan remained silent the rest of the way. When they had arrived at the mud road, however, he said slowly:

'I don't think that the expensive ring proves that the man was rich, sir. Vagrant crooks are very superstitious as a rule.

They will often hang on to a piece of stolen jewellery, just because they believe it brings them good luck.'

'Quite. Well, I'll go and change now, for I am wet all over. You'll find me presently, in my private office.'

After Judge Dee had taken a bath and changed into his ceremonial robe of green brocade, he had just time for one cup of tea. Then Tao Gan helped him to put the black winged judge's cap on his head, and they went together to the court-hall, adjoining Judge Dee's private office. Only a few routine matters came up, so the judge could rap his gavel and close the session after only half an hour. Back in his private office, he seated himself behind his large writing-desk, pushed the pile of official documents aside and placed the emerald ring before him. Then he took his folding fan from his sleeve and said, pointing with it at the ring:

'A queer case, Tao Gan! What could those cut-off fingers mean? That the murderer tortured his victim prior to killing him, in order to make him tell something? Or did he cut the fingers off after the murder, because they bore some mark or other that might prove the dead man's identity?'

Tao Gan did not reply at once. He poured a cup of hot tea for the judge, then sat down again on the stool in front of the desk and began, slowly pulling at the three long hairs that sprouted from his left cheek:

'Since the four fingers seem to have been cut off together with one blow, I think your second supposition is right, sir. According to our headman, that deserted hut was often used by vagabonds. Now, many of those vagrant ruffians are organized in regular gangs or secret brotherhoods. Every prospective member must swear an oath of allegiance to the leader of the gang and, as proof of his sincerity and his courage, himself solemnly cut off the tip of his left little finger. If this is indeed a gang murder, then the killers may

13

well have hacked off the four fingers in order to conceal the mutilation of the little finger, and thus destroy an important clue to the background of the crime.'

Judge Dee tapped his fan on the desk.

'Excellent reasoning, Tao Gan. Let's start by assuming that you are right. In that case . . .'

There was a knock on the door. The coroner came in and respectfully greeted the judge. He placed a filled-out official form on the desk and said:

'This is my autopsy report, Your Honour. I have written in all details, except the name, of course. The deceased must have been about fifty years old, and he was apparently in good health. I didn't find either any bodily defects, or larger birthmarks or scars. There were no bruises or other signs of violence. He was killed by one blow on the back of his head, presumably from an iron hammer, small but heavy. Four fingers of the left hand have been chopped off, either directly before or after the murder. He must have been killed late last night.'

The coroner scratched his head, then resumed somewhat diffidently:

'I must confess that I am rather puzzled by those missing fingers, sir. I could not make out how exactly they were cut off. The bones of the remaining stumps are not crushed, the flesh along the cuts is not bruised, and the skin shows no ragged ends. The hand must have been spread out on a flat surface, then all four fingers chopped off at the same time by one blow of some heavy, razor-edged cutting tool. If it had been done with a large axe, or a two-handed sword, one would never have obtained that perfectly straight, clean cut. I really don't know what to think!'

Judge Dee glanced through the report. Looking up, he asked the coroner:

'What about his feet?'

'Their condition pointed to a tramp, sir. Callosities in the usual places, and torn toenails. The feet of a man who walks a great deal, often barefooted.'

'I see. Did anybody recognize him?'

'No sir. I was present while the personnel of the tribunal filed past the dead body. Nobody had ever seen him before.'

'Thank you. You may go.'

The headman, who had been waiting in the corridor till the interview was over, now came in and reported that Mr Wang, the pharmacist, had arrived.

Judge Dee closed his fan. 'Show him in!' he ordered the headman.

The pharmacist was a small, dapper man with a slight stoop, very neatly dressed in a robe of black silk and square black cap. He had a pale, rather reserved face, marked by a jet-black moustache and goatee. After he had made his bow, Judge Dee told him affably:

'Do sit down, Mr Wang! We are not in the tribunal here. I am sorry to disturb you, but I need some information on the situation up on the ridge. During the daytime you are always in your shop in the market-place, of course, but I assume that you pass the evening and night in your mountain villa?'

'Yes indeed, Your Honour,' Wang replied in a cultured, measured voice. 'It's much cooler up there than here in town, this time of year.'

'Precisely. I heard that some ruffians created a disturbance up there last night.'

'No, everything was quiet last night, sir. It is true that all kinds of tramps and other riff-raff are about there. They pass the night in the forest, because they are afraid to enter the city at a late hour when the nightwatch might arrest them. The presence of those scoundrels is the only drawback of that otherwise most desirable neighbourhood. Sometimes we hear them shout and quarrel on the road, but all the villas there, including mine, have a high outer wall, so we need not be afraid of attempts at robbery, and we just ignore them.'

'I would appreciate it if you would also ask your servants, Mr Wang. The disturbance may not have taken place on the highway, but behind your house, in the wood.'

'I can inform Your Honour now that they haven't seen or heard anything. I was at home the entire evening, and none of us went out. You might ask Mr Leng, the pawn-broker, sir. He lives next door, and he . . . he keeps rather irregular hours.'

'Who else is living there, Mr Wang?'

'At the moment nobody, sir. There are three more villas, but those belong to wealthy merchants from the capital who come for their summer holiday only. All three are standing empty now.'

'I see. Well, thanks very much, Mr Wang. Would you mind going to the mortuary with the headman? I want you to have a look at the dead body of a vagabond, and let me know whether you have seen him in your neighbourhood lately.'

After the pharmacist had taken his leave with a low bow, Tao Gan said:

'We must also reckon with the possibility that the man was murdered here in town, sir. In a winehouse or in a low-class brothel.'

Judge Dee shook his head.

'If that had been the case, Tao Gan, they would have hidden the body under the floor, or thrown it in a dry well. They would never have dared take the risk of conveying it to the mountain slope, for then they would have been obliged to pass close by this tribunal.' He took the ring from his sleeve again and handed it to Tao Gan. 'When the coroner came in, I was just about to ask you to go down into the town and show this ring around in the small pawnshops there. You can do so now. You needn't worry about the routine of the chancery, Tao Gan! I shall take care of that, this morning.'

He dismissed his lieutenant with an encouraging smile, then he began to sort out the official correspondence that had come in that morning. He had the dossiers he needed fetched from the archives, and set to work. He was disturbed only once, when the headman came in to report that Mr Wang had viewed the body and stated that he did not recognize the dead tramp.

At noon the judge sent for a tray with rice-gruel and salted vegetables and ate at his desk, attended upon by one of the chancery clerks. While sipping a cup of strong tea he went over in his mind the case of the murdered vagabond. He slowly shook his head. Although the facts that had come to light thus far pointed to a gang murder, he was still groping for another approach. He had to admit, however, that his doubts rested on flimsy grounds: just his impression that the dead man had not been a tramp, but an educated, intelligent man, and of a strong character. He decided that for the time being he would not communicate his indecision to his lieutenant. Tao Gan had been in his service only ten months, and he was so eager that the judge felt reluctant to discourage him by questioning the validity of his theory about the significance of the missing four fingers. And it would be very wrong to teach him to go by hunches rather than by facts!

With a sigh Judge Dee set his teacup down and pulled a bulky dossier towards him. It contained all the papers relating to the smuggling case in the neighbouring district of Chiang-pei. Four days before, the military police had surprised three men who were trying to get two boxes across the river that formed the boundary between the two districts. The men had fled into the woods of Chiang-pei, leaving the boxes behind. They proved to be crammed with small packages containing gold and silver dust, camphor, mercury, and *ginseng*—the costly medicinal root imported from Korea— and all these goods were subject to a heavy road-tax. Since the seizure had taken place in Chiang-pei, the case concerned Judge Dee's colleague, the magistrate of that district. But he happened to be short-handed and had requested Judge Dee's assistance. The judge had agreed at once, all the more readily since he suspected that the smugglers had accomplices in his own district. He had sent his trusted old adviser Sergeant Hoong to Chiang-pei, together with his two lieutenants Ma Joong and Chiao Tai. They had established their headquarters in the military guardpost, at the bridge that crossed the boundary river.

The judge took the sketchmap of the region from the file, and studied it intently. Ma Joong and Chiao Tai had scoured the woods with the military police, and interrogated the peasants living in the fields beyond, without discovering a single clue. It was an awkward affair, for the higher authorities always took a grave view of evasion of the road-taxes. The Prefect, the direct superior of Judge Dee and his colleague of Chiang-pei, had sent the latter a peremptory note, stating that he expected quick results. He had added that the matter was urgent, for the large amount and the high cost of the contraband proved that it had not been an incidental attempt by local smugglers. They must have a powerful organization behind them that directed the operations. The three smugglers were only important in so far as they could give a lead to the identity of their principal. The metropolitan authorities suspected that a leading financier in the capital was the ringleader. If this master-criminal was not tracked down, the smuggling would continue.

Shaking his head the judge poured himself another cup of tea.

Tao Gan came back to the market-place dog-tired and in a very bad temper. In the hot and smelly quarter behind the fishmarket down town, he had visited no less than six pawnshops and made exhaustive enquiries in a number of small gold and silver shops, and also in a few disreputable hostels and dosshouses. Nobody had ever seen an emerald ring with two entwined dragons, nor heard about a gang fight in or outside the city.

He went up the broad stone steps of the Temple of Confucius, crowded with the stalls of street-vendors, and sat down on the bamboo stool in front of the stand of an oilcake hawker. Rubbing his sore legs he reflected sadly that he had failed in the first assignment Judge Dee had given him to carry out alone; for up to now he had always worked together with Ma Joong and Chiao Tai. He had lost this rare chance of proving his mettle! 'It's true,' he told himself, 'that I lack the physical strength and experience in detecting of my colleagues, but I know as much as they about the ways and byways of the underworld, if not more! Why . . . ?'

'This place is meant for business, not for taking a gratis rest!' the cake vendor told him sourly. 'Besides, your long face keeps other customers away!'

Tao Gan gave him a dirty look and invested five coppers in a handful of oilcakes. Those would have to do for his luncheon for he was a very parsimonious man. Munching the cakes, he let his eyes rove over the market-place. He bestowed an envious look upon the beautiful front of Wang's pharmacy over on the other side, lavishly decorated with gold lacquer. The tall greystone building next door looked simple but dignified. Over the barred windows hung a small signboard reading 'Leng's Pawnshop'.

'Vagabonds wouldn't patronize such a high-class pawn-shop,' Tao Gan muttered. 'But since I am here anyway, I might as well have a look there too. And Leng has a villa on the ridge. He may have heard or seen something last night.' He rose and elbowed his way through the market crowd.

About a dozen neatly dressed customers were standing in front of the high counter that ran across the high, spacious room, talking busily with the clerks. In the rear a large, fat man was sitting at a massive desk, working an enormous abacus with his white, podgy hands. He wore a wide grey robe, and a small black cap. Tao Gan reached into his capacious sleeve and handed to the nearest clerk an impressive red visiting-card. It bore in large letters the inscription 'Kan Tao, antique gold and silver bought and sold'. And in the corner the address: the famous street of jewellers in the capital. This was one of the many faked visiting-cards Tao Gan had used during his long career as a professional swindler; upon entering Judge Dee's service he had been unable to bring himself to do away with that choice collection.

When the clerk had shown the card to the fat man, he got up at once and came waddling to the counter. His round, haughty face was creased in a friendly smile when he asked:

'And what can we do for you today, sir?'

'I just want some confidential information, Mr Leng. A fellow offered me an emerald ring at only one-third of the value. I suspect it has been stolen, and was wondering whether someone might have tried to pawn it here.'

So speaking he took the ring from his sleeve and laid it on the counter.

Leng's face fell.

'No,' he replied curtly, 'never seen it before.' Then he snapped at the cross-eyed clerk who was peeping over his shoulder: 'None of your business!' To Tao Gan he added:

'Very sorry I can't help you, Mr Kan!' and went back to his desk.

The cross-eyed clerk winked at Tao Gan and pointed with his chin at the door. Tao Gan nodded and went outside. Seeing the red-marble bench in the porch of Wang's pharmacy next door, he sat there to wait.

Through the open window he watched with interest what was going on inside. Two shop assistants were turning pills between wooden disks, another was slicing a thick medicinal root on an iron chopping-board by means of the huge cleaver attached to it by a hinge. Two of their colleagues were sorting out dried centipedes and spiders; Tao Gan knew that these substances, pounded in a mortar together with the exuviae of cicadas and then dissolved in warm wine, made an excellent cough medicine.

Suddenly he heard footsteps. The cross-eyed clerk came up to him and sat down by his side.

'That thick-skulled boss of mine didn't recognize you,' the clerk said with a self-satisfied smirk, 'but I placed you at once! I remember clearly having seen you in the tribunal, sitting at the table of the clerks!'

'Come to the point!' Tao Gan told him crossly.

'The point is that the fat bastard lied, my dear friend! He had seen that ring before. Had it in his hands, at the counter.'

'Well, well. He has forgotten all about it, I suppose.'

'Not on your life! That ring was brought to us two days ago, by a damned good-looking girl. Just as I was going to ask her whether she wanted to pawn it, the boss comes up and pushes me away. He is always after pretty young women, the old goat! Well, I watched them, but I couldn't hear what they were whispering about. Finally the wench picks up the ring again, and off she went.'

'What kind of a woman was she?'

21

'Not a lady, that I can tell you! Dressed in a patched blue jacket and trousers, like a scullery maid. Holy heaven, if I were rich I wouldn't mind having a maid like that about the house, not a bit! Wasn't she a stunner! Anyway, my boss is a crook, I tell you. He's mixed up in all kinds of shady deals, and he also cheats with his taxes.'

'You don't seem very fond of your boss.'

'You should know how he's sweating us! And he and that snooty son of his keep their eyes on me and my colleagues all the time, fat chance we have to make any money on the side!' The clerk heaved a deep sigh, then resumed, business-like: 'If the tribunal pays me ten coppers a day, I shall collect evidence on his tax evasion. For the information I gave you just now, twenty-five coppers will do.'

Tao Gan rose and patted the other's shoulder.

'Carry on, my boy!' he told him cheerfully. 'Then you'll also become a big fat bully in due time, working an enormous abacus.' Then he added sternly: 'If I need you I'll send for you. Good-bye!'

The disappointed clerk scurried back to the pawn shop. Tao Gan followed him at a more sedate pace. Inside he rapped on the counter with his bony knuckles and peremptorily beckoned the portly pawnbroker. Showing him his identity document bearing the large red stamp of the tribunal, he told him curtly:

'You'll have to come with me to the tribunal, Mr Leng. His Excellency the magistrate wants to see you. No, there is no need to change. That grey dress of yours is very becoming. Hurry up, I don't have all day!'

They were carried to the tribunal in Leng's luxurious padded palankeen.

Tao Gan told the pawnbroker to wait in the chancery. Leng let himself down heavily on the bench in the ante-room and at once began to fan himself vigorously with a large silk fan. He jumped up when Tao Gan came to fetch him.

'What is it all about, sir?' he asked worriedly.

Tao Gan gave him a pitying look. He was thoroughly enjoying himself.

'Well,' he said slowly, 'I can't talk about official business, of course. But I'll say this much: I am glad I am not in your shoes, Mr Leng!'

When the sweating pawnbroker was ushered in by Tao Gan into Judge Dee's office, and he saw the judge sitting behind his desk, he fell onto his knees and began to knock his forehead on the floor.

'You may skip the formalities, Mr Leng!' Judge Dee told him coldly. 'Sit down and listen! It is my duty to warn you that if you don't answer my questions truthfully, I shall have to interrogate you in court. Speak up, where were you last night?'

'Merciful Heaven! So it is just as I feared!' the fat man exclaimed. 'It was just that I had had a few drops too much, Excellency! I swear it! When I was closing up, my old friend Chu the goldsmith dropped in and invited me to have a drink in the winehouse on the corner. We had two jugs, sir! At the most! I was still steady on my legs. The old man told you that, I suppose?'

Judge Dee nodded. He didn't have the faintest idea what the excited man was talking about. If Leng had said he was at home the previous night the judge had planned to ask him whether there had been a commotion on the ridge, and then he would have confronted him with his lying about the emerald ring. Now he told him curtly: 'I want to hear everything again, from your own mouth!'

'Well, after I had taken leave of my friend Chu, Excellency, I told my palankeen bearers to carry me up to my villa on the ridge. When we were rounding the corner of your tribunal here, a band of young rascals, grown-up gutter-snipes, began to jeer at me. As a rule I don't pay any attention to that kind of thing, but . . . well, as I said, I was... Anyway, I got angry and told my bearers to put the palankeen down and teach the scum a lesson. Then suddenly that old vagabond appears. He kicks against my palankeen and starts calling me a dirty tyrant. Well, I mean a man in my position can't take that lying down! I step from my palankeen and I give the old scoundrel a push. Just a push, Excellency. He falls down, and remains lying there on his back.'

The pawnbroker produced a large silk handkerchief and rubbed his moist face.

'Did his head bleed?' the judge asked.

'Bleed? Of course not, sir! He fell on to the soft shoulder of the mud road. But I should've had a good look, of course, to see whether he was all right. However, those young hoodlums began to shout again, so I jumped in my palankeen and told the bearers to carry me away. It was only when I was about half-way up the road to the ridge, and when the evening breeze had cooled my head a bit, that I realized that the old tramp might have had a heart attack. So I stepped out and told the bearers that I would walk a bit and that they could go on ahead to the villa. Then I walked downhill, back to the place of the quarrel. But . . .'

'Why didn't you simply tell your chair-bearers to take you back there?' Judge Dee interrupted.

The pawnbroker looked embarrassed.

'Well, sir, you know what those coolies are nowadays. If that tramp had really fallen ill, I wouldn't want my bearers to know that, you see. Those impudent rascals aren't beyond trying a bit of blackmail. . . . Anyway, when I came to the street corner here, the old tramp was nowhere to be seen. A hawker told me that the old scoundrel had scrambled up

24

again shortly after I had left. He had said some very bad things about me, then he took the road to the ridge, as chipper as can be!'

'I see. What did you do next?'

'I? Oh, I rented a chair, and was carried home. But the incident had upset my stomach, and when I descended in front of my gate, I suddenly became very ill. Fortunately Mr Wang and his son were just coming back from a walk, and his son carried me inside. Strong as an ox, that boy is. Well, then I went straight to bed.' He again mopped his face before he concluded: 'I fully realized that I shouldn't have laid hands on that old vagabond, Excellency. And now he has lodged a complaint, of course. Well, I am prepared to pay any indemnity, within reason, of course, and . . .'

Judge Dee had risen.

'Come with me, Mr Leng,' he said evenly. 'I want to show you something.'

The judge left the office, followed by Tao Gan and the bewildered pawnbroker. In the courtyard the judge told the headman to take them to the mortuary in the gatehouse. He led them to a musty room, bare except for a deal table on trestles, covered with a reed mat. The judge lifted up the end of the mat, and asked:

'Do you know this man, Mr Leng?'

After one look at the old tramp's face, Leng shouted:

'He is dead! Holy Heaven, I killed him!'

He fell on his knees and wailed: 'Mercy, Excellency, have mercy! It was an accident, I swear it! I . . .'

'You'll be given an opportunity to explain when you are standing trial,' Judge Dee told him coldly. 'Now we'll go back to my office, for I am not yet through with you, Mr Leng. Not by a long shot!'

Back in his private office the judge sat down behind his desk and motioned Tao Gan to take the stool in front. Leng was not invited to be seated so he had to remain standing there, under the watchful eye of the headman.

Judge Dee silently studied him for a while, slowly caressing his long sidewhiskers. Then he sat up, took the emerald ring from his sleeve and asked:

'Why did you tell my assistant that you had never seen this ring before?'

Leng stared at the ring with raised eyebrows. He did not seem much disturbed by Judge Dee's sudden question.

'I couldn't have known that this gentleman belonged to the tribunal, could I, sir?' he asked, annoyed. 'Otherwise I would have told him, of course. But the ring reminded me of a rather unpleasant experience, and I didn't feel like discussing that with a complete stranger.'

'All right. Now tell me who that young woman was.'

Leng shrugged his round shoulders.

'I really couldn't tell you, sir! She was dressed rather poorly, and she belonged to a band of vagabonds for the tip of her little finger was missing. But a good-looking wench. Very good-looking, I must say. Well, she puts the ring on the table and asks what it's worth. It's a nice antique piece, as you can see for yourself, sir, worth about six silver pieces. Ten, perhaps, to a collector. So I tell her, "I can let you have here and now one good shining silver piece if you want to pawn it, and two if you sell it outright." Business is business, isn't it? Even if your customer happens to be a pretty piece of goods. But does she take my offer? No sir! She snatches the ring from my hands, snaps "Not for sale!" and off she goes. And that was the last I saw of her.'

'I heard a quite different story,' Judge Dee said dryly. 'Speak up, what were you two whispering about?'

Leng's face turned red.

'So my clerks, those good-for-nothings, have been spying on me again! Well, then you'll understand how awkward

'I AM NOT YET THROUGH WITH YOU, MR LENG!'

it was, sir. I asked her only because I thought that such a good-looking girl from up-country, all alone in this town ... well, that she might meet the wrong people, and . . .'

Judge Dee hit his fist on the table.

'Don't stand there twaddling, man! Tell me exactly what you said!'

'Well,' Leng replied with a sheepish look, 'I proposed that we should meet later in a tea-house near by, and . . . and I patted her hand a bit, just to assure her I meant well, you know. The wench suddenly flew into a rage, said that if I didn't stop bothering her, she would call her brother who was waiting outside. Then . . . then she rushed off.'

'Quite. Headman, put this man under lock and key. The charge is manslaughter.'

The headman grabbed the protesting pawnbroker and took him outside.

'Pour me another cup of tea, Tao Gan,' Judge Dee said. 'A curious story! And did you notice the discrepancy between Leng's account of his meeting with the girl and that given by the clerk?'

'I did, sir!' Tao Gan said eagerly. That wretched clerk said nothing about their having a quarrel at the counter. According to him they held a whispered conversation. I think that in fact the girl accepted Leng's proposal, sir. The quarrel Leng spoke of occurred afterwards, in the house of assignation. And that is why Leng murdered the old tramp!'

Judge Dee, who had been slowly sipping his tea, now put his cup down. Leaning back in his chair, he said:

'Develop your theory further, Tao Gan!'

'Well, this time Leng's philandering led to serious trouble! For the girl, her brother and the old tramp belonged to one and the same organized gang; the girl was their call bird. As soon as Leng had arrived in the house of assignation and began to make up to the girl, she shouted that he was assaulting her—the old, familiar trick. Her brother and the old tramp came rushing inside, and demanded money. Leng succeeded in escaping. When he was on his way to the ridge, however, the old tramp waylaid him and tried to make Leng pay up by making a scene in the street. Leng's bearers were beating up the young hoodlums, so they couldn't hear what Leng and the old man were quarrelling about. Leng silenced the tramp by knocking him down. What do you think of that as a theory, sir?'

'Plausible, and in perfect accordance with Leng's character. Continue!'

'While Leng was being carried up to the ridge he did indeed become worried. Not about the condition of the old tramp, however, but about the other members of the gang. He was afraid that when they found the old tramp, they would come after him to take revenge. When the hawker told Leng that the tramp had taken the road uphill, Leng followed him. About half-way up he struck him down from behind, with a sharp piece of rock, or perhaps the hilt of his dagger.'

Tao Gan paused. When the judge nodded encouragingly, he resumed:

'It was comparatively easy for Leng, who is a powerful fellow and perfectly familiar with that area, to carry the dead body to the deserted hut. And Leng also had a good reason for cutting off his victim's fingers, namely to hide the fact that the man was a member of a gang. But as to where and how Leng cut off the fingers, I confess that that is a complete riddle to me, sir.'

Judge Dee sat up straight. Stroking his long black beard, he said with a smile:

'You did very well indeed. You have a logical mind, and at the same time strong powers of imagination, a combination that'll go a long way to make you a good investigator! I shall certainly keep your theory in mind. However, its weak point is that it is based entirely on the assumption that the eyewitness account of the clerk regarding the meeting in the pawnshop is absolutely correct. But when I mentioned the discrepancy between the two accounts just now, my intention was to quote it as an example of how little trust can be put in eyewitness accounts. As a matter of fact, it is too early yet to formulate theories, Tao Gan. First we must verify the facts we have, and try to discover additional data.'

Noticing Tao Gan's crestfallen look, Judge Dee went on quickly:

'Thanks to your excellent work this afternoon, we now have at our disposal three well-established facts. First, that a beautiful vagabond girl is connected with the ring. Second, that she has a brother; for no matter what really happened, Leng had no earthly reason to invent a brother. And third, that there is a connection between the girl, her brother and the murdered man. Probably they belonged to the same gang, and if so, it probably was a gang from outside this district; for none of our personnel knew the dead man by sight, and Leng thought the girl was from up-country.

'So now your next step is to locate the girl and her brother. That shouldn't be too difficult, for a vagabond girl of such striking beauty will attract attention. As a rule the women who join those gangs are cheap prostitutes.'

'I could ask the Chief of the Beggars, sir! He is a clever old scoundrel, and fairly co-operative.'

'Yes, that's a good idea. While you are busy in the town, I shall check Leng's story. I shall interrogate that rascally clerk of his, his friend the goldsmith Chu, and his chair-bearers. I shall also order the headman to locate one or more of the young hoodlums who jeered at Leng, and the hawker who saw the old man scramble up. Finally I shall ask Mr Wang whether Leng was really dead drunk when he came home. All these routine jobs would be meat and drink to old Hoong, Ma Joong and Chiao Tai, but since they are away I'll gladly take care of them myself. This work will help to take my mind off that smuggling case that is worrying me considerably. Well, set to work, and success!'

The only occupant of the smelly taproom of the Red Carp was the greybeard who stood behind the high counter. He wore a long, shabby blue gown, and had a greasy black skull cap on his head. His long, wrinkled face was adorned by a ragged moustache and a spiky chinbeard. Staring into the distance he was moodily picking his broken teeth. His busy time would come late in the night, when his beggars gathered there in order to pay him his share of their earnings. The old man looked on silently while Tao Gan poured himself uninvited a cup of wine from the cracked earthenware pot. Then he quickly grabbed the pot, and put it away under the counter.

'You had quite a busy morning, Mr Tao,' he croaked. 'Asking about gang fights, and golden rings.'

Tao Gan nodded. He knew that the greybeard's omnipresent beggars kept him informed about everything that went on downtown. He put his wine-cup down and said cheerfully:

'That's why I got the afternoon off! I was thinking of amusing myself a bit. Not with a professional, mind you. With a free-lance!'

'Very clever!' the greybeard commented sourly. 'So as to turn her in afterwards for practising without a licence. Have your fun gratis, and on top of that a bonus from the tribunal!'

'What do you take me for? I want a free-lance, and from out of town, because I have to think of my reputation.'

'Why should you, Mr Tao?' the Chief of the Beggars asked blandly. 'Your reputation being what it is?'

31

Tao Gan decided to let the barbed remark pass. He said pensively:

'Something young, and pretty. But cheap, mind you!'

'You'll have to prove that you'll appreciate my advice, Mr Tao!'

The greybeard watched Tao Gan as he laboriously counted out five coppers on the counter, but he made no move to take the money. With a deep sigh Tao Gan added five more. Now the old man scooped them up with his claw-like hand.

'Go to the Inn of the Blue Clouds,' he muttered. 'Two streets down, the fourth house on your left. Ask for Seng Kiu. He's her brother, and he concludes the deals, I am told.' He gave Tao Gan a thoughtful look, then added with a lopsided grin: 'You'll like Seng Kiu, Mr Tao! A straightforward, open-minded man. And very hospitable. Have a good time, Mr Tao. You really deserve it!'

Tao Gan thanked him and went out.

He walked as quickly as the irregular cobblestones of the narrow alley would allow, for he did not put it beyond the greybeard to send one of his beggars ahead to the inn to warn Seng Kiu that a minion of the law was on his way.

The Inn of the Blue Clouds was a miserable small place, wedged in between the shops of a fishmonger and a vegetable dealer. In the dimly lit space at the bottom of the narrow staircase a fat man sat dozing in a bamboo chair. Tao Gan poked him hard in his ribs with his thin, bony forefinger and growled:

'I want Seng Kiu!'

'You may have him and keep him! Upstairs, second door! Ask him when he's going to pay the rent!' When Tao Gan was about to ascend, the man, who had taken in his frail stooping figure, called out: 'Wait! Have a look at my face!'

Tao Gan saw that his left eye was closed, the cheek swollen and discoloured.

'That's Seng Kiu for you!' the man said. 'Mean bastard!'

'How many are they?'

'Three. Besides Seng Kiu and his sister there's his friend Chang. Also a mean bastard. There was a fourth, but he has cleared out.'

Tao Gan nodded. While climbing the stairs he reflected with a wry smile that he now knew the reason for the greybeard's secret amusement. He would get even with that old rascal, some day!

After he had rapped his knuckles vigorously on the door indicated, a raucous voice called out from inside:

'Tomorrow you'll get your money, you son of a dog!'

Tao Gan pushed the door open and walked inside. On either side of the bare, dingy room stood a plank-bed. On the one on the right lay a giant of a man, clad in a patched brown jacket and trousers. He had a broad, bloated face, surrounded by a bristling short beard. His hair was bound up with a dirty rag. On the other bed a long, wiry man lay snoring loudly, his muscular arms folded under his closely-cropped head. In front of the window sat a good-looking young woman mending a jacket. She wore only a pair of wide blue trousers, her shapely torso was bare.

'Maybe I could help with the rent, Seng Kiu,' Tao Gan said. He pointed with his chin at the girl.

The giant scrambled up. He looked Tao Gan up and down with his small bloodshot eyes, scratching his hairy breast. Tao Gan noticed that the tip of his left little finger was missing. His scrutiny completed, the giant asked gruffly: 'How much?'

'Fifty coppers.'

Seng Kiu woke up the other by a kick against his leg that was dangling over the foot of the bed.

'This kind old gentleman,' he informed him, 'wants to lend us fifty coppers, because he likes our faces. The trouble is that I don't like his!'

'Take his money and kick him out!' the girl told her brother. 'No need to beat him up, the scarecrow is ugly enough as it is!'

The giant swung round to her.

'None of your business!' he barked. 'You shut up and stay shut up! You bungled that affair with Uncle Twan, couldn't even get that emerald ring of his! Useless slut!'

She came to her feet with amazing speed and kicked him hard against his shins. He promptly gave her a blow to her stomach. She folded double, gasping for air. But that was only a trick, for when he came for her, she quickly thrust her head into his midriff. As he stepped back, she pulled a long hairpin from her coiffure and asked venomously:

'Want to get that into your gut, dear brother?'

Tao Gan was thinking how he could get these three to the tribunal. Since they probably weren't very familiar with the city yet, he thought he would manage it.

'I'll settle with you later!' Seng Kiu promised his sister. And to his friend: 'Grab the bastard, Chang!'

While Chang was keeping Tao Gan's arms pinned behind his back in an iron grip, Seng Kiu expertly searched him.

'Yes, only fifty coppers!' he said with disgust. 'You hold him while I teach him not to disturb our sleep!'

He took a long bamboo stick from the corner and made to hit Tao Gan on his head. But suddenly he half turned and let the end come down on the behind of his sister, who was bending over her jacket again. She jumped aside with a yell of pain. Her brother bellowed with laughter. But then he had to duck, for she threw the heavy iron scissors at his head.

'I don't like interrupting,' Tao Gan said dryly, 'but there's a deal of five silver pieces I wanted to discuss.'

'IT'S A VERY PRIVATE MATTER,' TAO GAN SAID

The giant who had been trying to get hold of his sister now let her go. He turned round and asked panting:

'Five silver pieces, you said?'

'It's a very private matter, just between you and me.'

Seng Kiu gave a sign to Chang to let Tao Gan go. The thin man drew the tall ruffian into the corner and told him in a low voice:

'I don't care a fig about that sister of yours. It's my boss who sent me!'

Seng Kiu went pale under his tan.

'Does the Baker want five silver pieces? Holy Heaven, has he gone mad? How . . .?'

'I don't know any baker,' Tao Gan said crossly. 'My boss is a big landowner, a wealthy lecher who pays well for his little amusements. He has got fed up with all those dainty damsels from the Willow Quarter nowadays. Suddenly he wants them buxom and rough-and-ready like. I do the collecting for him. He has heard about your sister, and he has sent me to offer you five silver pieces for having her in the house a couple of days.'

Seng Kiu had been listening with growing astonishment. Now he exclaimed:

'Are you crazy? There isn't a woman in the whole wide world who has got something to sell worth that much!' He thought deeply for a while, creasing his low forehead. Suddenly he burst out: 'That proposal of yours stinks, brother! I want my sister to keep a whole skin. I am planning to set her up in business, you see? So she gets me a regular income.'

Tao Gan shrugged his narrow shoulders.

'All right. There are other vagabond girls on the loose. Give me back my fifty coppers, then I'll say good-bye.'

'Hey there, not so fast!' The giant rubbed his face. 'Five silver pieces! That means living nicely for at least a year, without doing a stroke of work! Well, it doesn't matter much really whether she's handled a bit roughly, after all. She can stand a lot, and it'll cut her down to size, maybe. All right, it's a deal! But me and Chang are going to see her off. I want to know where and with whom she is staying.'

'So that you can blackmail my boss later, eh? Nothing doing!'

'You are lying! You are a buyer for a brothel, you dirty rat!'

'All right, come with me then and see for yourself. But don't blame me if my boss gets angry and has his men beat you up. Pay me twenty coppers, that's my commission.'

After protracted haggling, they agreed on ten coppers. Seng Kiu gave Tao Gan his fifty coppers back, and ten extra. The gaunt man put these in his sleeve with a satisfied smile, for now he had recovered the money he had paid the Chief of the Beggars.

'The boss of this fellow wants to stand us a drink,' Seng Kiu told Chang and his sister. 'Let's go to his place and hear what he has got to say.'

They went up town by the main road, but then Tao Gan took them through a maze of narrow alleys to the back of a tall greystone compound. As he opened the small iron door with a key he took from his sleeve, Seng Kiu remarked, impressed:

'Your boss must be rolling in it! Substantial property!'

'Very substantial,' Tao Gan agreed. 'And this is only the back entrance, mind you. You should see the main gate!' So speaking, he herded them into a long corridor. He carefully relocked the door and said: 'Just wait here a moment while I go to inform my boss!'

He disappeared round the corner.

After a while the girl exclaimed:

37

'I don't like the smell of this place. Could be a trap!'

Then the headman and six armed guards came tramping round the corner. Chang cursed and groped for his knife.

'Please attack us!' the headman told him with a grin, raising his sword. 'Then we'll get a bonus for cutting you down!'

'Leave it, Chang!' the giant told his friend disgustedly. 'These bastards are professional murderers. They get paid for killing the poor!'

The girl tried to slip past the headman, but he caught her and soon she also was in chains. They were taken to the jail in the adjoining building.

After Tao Gan had run to the guardhouse and told the headman to arrest two vagabonds and their wench who were waiting near the back door, he went straight to the chancery and asked the senior clerk where he could find Judge Dee.

'His Excellency is in his office, Mr. Tao. Since the noon rice he has interrogated a number of people there. Just when he had let them go, young Mr Leng, the son of the pawnbroker, came and asked to see the judge. He hasn't come out yet.'

'What is that youngster doing here? He wasn't on the list of people the judge wanted to interrogate.'

'I think he came to find out why his father had been arrested, Mr Tao. It might interest you to know that, before he went inside, he had been asking the guards at the gate all kinds of questions about the dead body that was found this morning in the hut in the forest. You might tell the judge.'

'Thank you, I will. Those guards are not supposed to hand out information, though!'

The old clerk shrugged his shoulders.

'They all know young Mr Leng, sir. They often go there towards the end of the month to pawn something or other, and young Leng always gives them a square deal. Besides, since the entire personnel has seen the body, it isn't much of a secret any more.'

Tao Gan nodded and walked on to Judge Dee's office.

The judge was sitting behind his desk, now wearing a comfortable robe of thin grey cotton, and with a square black cap on his head. In front of the desk stood a well-built young man of about twenty-five, clad in a neat brown robe and wearing a flat black cap. He had a handsome but rather reserved face.

'Take a seat!' Judge Dee told Tao Gan. 'This is Mr Leng's eldest son. He is worried about his father's arrest. I just explained to him that I suspect his father of having taken part in the murder of an old vagrant, and that I shall hear the case at tonight's session of the court. That's all I can say, Mr Leng. I have to terminate our interview now, for I have urgent matters to discuss with my lieutenant here.'

'My father couldn't possibly have committed a murder last night, sir,' the youngster said quietly.

Judge Dee raised his eyebrows.

'Why?'

'For the simple reason that my father was dead drunk, sir. I myself opened the door when Mr Wang brought him in. My father had passed out, and Mr Wang's son had to carry him inside.'

'All right, Mr Leng. I shall keep this point in mind.'

Young Leng made no move to take his leave. He cleared his throat and resumed, rather diffidently this time:

'I think I have seen the murderers, sir.'

Judge Dee leaned forward in his chair.

'I want a complete statement about that!' he said sharply.

'Well, sir, it is rumoured that the dead body of a tramp was found this morning in a deserted hut in the forest, half-way up the slope. May I ask whether that is correct?' As the judge nodded, he continued: 'Last night a bright moon was in the sky and there was a cool evening breeze, so I thought I would take a little walk. I took the footpath behind our house that leads down into the forest. After having passed the second bend, I saw two people some distance ahead of me. I couldn't see them very well, but one seemed very tall, and he was carrying a heavy load on his shoulders. The other was small, and rather slender. Since all kind of riff-raff often frequents the forest at night, I decided to call off my walk, and went back home. When I heard the rumour about the dead tramp, it occurred to me that the burden the tall person was carrying might well have been the dead body.'

Tao Gan tried to catch Judge Dee's eye, for Leng's description fitted exactly Seng Kiu and his sister. But the judge was looking intently at his visitor. Suddenly he said:

'This means that I can set your father free at once, and arrest you as suspect in his stead! For you have just proved beyond doubt that, whereas your father could not have committed the murder, you yourself had every opportunity!'

The youngster stared dumbfounded at the judge.

'I didn't do it!' he burst out. 'I can prove it! I have a witness who . . .'

'Just as I thought! You weren't alone. A young man like you doesn't go out for a solitary walk in the forest at night. It's only when you have reached a riper age that you discover that enjoyment. Speak up, who was the girl?'

'My mother's chambermaid,' the young man replied with a red face. 'We can't see much of each other inside the house, of course. So we meet now and then in the hut, down the slope. She can bear out my statement that we went into the forest together, but she can't give more information about the people I saw, because I was walking ahead and she didn't see them.' Giving the judge a shy look he added:

'We plan to get married, sir. But if my father knew that we . . .'

'All right. Go to the chancery, and let the senior clerk take down your statement. I shall use it only if absolutely necessary. You may go!'

As the youngster made to take his leave, Tao Gan asked:

'Could that smaller figure you saw have been a girl?'

Young Leng scratched his head.

'Well, I couldn't see them very well, you know. Now that you ask me, however . . . Yes, it might have been a woman, I think.'

As soon as young Leng had gone, Tao Gan began excitedly:

'Everything is clear now, sir! I . . .'

Judge Dee raised his hand.

'One moment, Tao Gan. We must deal with this complicated case methodically. I shall first tell you the result of my routine check. First, that clerk of Leng's is a disgusting specimen. Close questioning proved that, after he had seen the girl place the ring on the counter, Leng told him to make himself scarce. Other customers came in between them, and later he only saw the girl snatch up the ring and go out. The whispering bit he made up, in order to prove that his boss is a lecher. And as to his boss being guilty of tax-evasion, he could only quote vague rumours. I dismissed the fellow with the reminder that there's a law on slander, and sent for the master of the Bankers' Guild. He told me that Mr Leng is a very wealthy man who likes to do himself well. He is not averse to a bit of double-dealing, and one has to look sharp when doing business with him, but he is careful to keep on the right side of the law. He travels a lot, however, passing much of his time in the neighbouring district of Chiang-pei; and the guildmaster did not, of course,

41

know anything about his activities there. Second, Leng did indeed have a heavy drinking bout with his friend the goldsmith. Third, the headman has located two of the young hoodlums who jeered at Leng. They said that this was obviously the first time Leng had seen the old tramp, and that no girl was mentioned during their quarrel. Leng did push the old man, but he was on his feet again directly after Leng had been carried off in his chair. He stood there cursing Leng for a blasted tyrant, then he walked off. Finally, those boys made one curious remark. They said that the old man didn't speak like a tramp at all, he used the language of a gentleman. I had planned to ask Mr Wang whether Mr Leng was really drunk when he came home, but after what his son told us just now, that doesn't seem necessary any more.'

The judge emptied his teacup, then added: 'Tell me now how it went down town!'

'I must first tell you, sir, that young Leng questioned the guards thoroughly about the discovery of the body in the hut, prior to seeing you. However, that seems immaterial now, for I have proof that he did not make up the story about the two people he saw in the forest.'

Judge Dee nodded.

'I didn't think he was lying. The boy impressed me as very honest. Much better than that father of his!'

'The people he saw must have been a gangster called Seng Kiu, and his sister—a remarkably beautiful young girl. The Chief of the Beggars directed me to the inn where they were staying, together with another plug-ugly called Chang. There was a fourth man, but he had left. I heard Seng Kiu scolding his sister for having spoiled what he called "the affair of Uncle Twan", and for having failed to obtain his emerald ring. Evidently that Uncle Twan is our dead tramp. All three are from another district, but they know a gangster boss called the Baker here. I had them locked up in jail, all three of them.'

'Excellent!' Judge Dee exclaimed. 'How did you get them here so quickly?'

'Oh,' Tao Gan replied vaguely, 'I told them a story about easy money to be made here, and they came along gladly. As to my theory about Mr Leng, sir, you were quite right in calling it premature! Leng had nothing to do with the murder. It was pure coincidence that the gangsters crossed his path twice. First when the girl wanted the ring appraised, and the second time when the old tramp took offence at Leng's high-handed way of dealing with the young hoodlums.'

The judge made no comment. He pensively tugged at his moustache. Suddenly he said:

'I don't like coincidences, Tao Gan. I admit they do occur, now and then. But I always begin by distrusting them. By the way, you said that Seng Kiu mentioned a gangster boss called the Baker. Before I interrogate him, I want you to ask our headman what he knows about that man.'

While Tao Gan was gone, the judge poured himself another cup from the tea basket on his desk. He idly wondered how his lieutenant had managed to get those three gangsters to the tribunal. 'He was remarkably vague when I asked him,' he told himself with a wry smile. 'Probably he has been acting the part of confidence man again—his old trade! Well, as long as it is in a good cause . . .'

Tao Gan came back.

'The headman knew the Baker quite well by name, sir. But he is not of this town; the scoundrel is a notorious gangster boss in our neighbouring district, Chiang-pei. That means that Seng Kiu is from there too.'

'And our friend Mr Leng often stays there,' the judge said slowly. 'We are getting too many coincidences for my liking, Tao Gan! Well, I shall interrogate those people separately, beginning with Seng Kiu. Tell the headman to take him to the mortuary—without showing him the dead body, of course. I'll go there presently.'

When Judge Dee came in he saw the tall figure of Seng Kiu standing between two constables, in front of the table on which the corpse was lying, covered by the reed mat. There hung a sickly smell in the bare room. The judge reflected that it wouldn't do to leave the body there too long, in this hot weather. He folded the mat back and asked Seng Kiu:

'Do you know this man?'

'Holy Heaven, that's him!' Seng shouted.

Judge Dee folded his arms in his wide sleeves. He spoke harshly:

'Yes, that's the dead body of the old man you cruelly did to death.'

The gangster burst out in a string of curses. The constable on his right hit him over his head with his heavy club. 'Confess!' he barked at him. The blow didn't seem to bother the giant much. He just shook his head, then shouted:

'I didn't kill him! The old fool was still alive and kicking when he left the inn last night!'

'Who was he?'

'A rich fool, called Twan Mou-tsai. Owned a big drugstore, in the capital.'

'A rich drug dealer? What was his business with you?'

'He was gone on my sister, the silly old goat! He wanted to join us!'

'Don't try to foist your stupid lies on me, my friend!' Judge Dee said coldly. The constable hit out at Seng Kiu's head again, but he ducked expertly and blurted out:

44

'It's the truth, I swear it! He was crazy about my sister! Even wanted to pay for being allowed to join us! But my sister, the silly wench, she wouldn't take one copper from him. And look at the trouble the stubborn little strumpet has got us in now! A murder, if you please!'

Judge Dee smoothed down his long beard. The man was an uncouth brute, but his words bore the hallmark of truth. Seng Kiu interpreted his silence as a sign of doubt, and resumed in a whining voice:

'Me and my mate, we have never done anything like murder, noble lord! Maybe we took along a stray chicken or a pig here and there, or borrowed a handful of coppers from a traveller—such things will happen when you have to make your living by the road. But we never killed a man, I tell you. And why should I kill Uncle Twan, of all people? I told you he gave me money, didn't I?'

'Is your sister a prostitute?'

'A what?' Seng Kiu asked suspiciously.

'A streetwalker.'

'Oh, that!' Seng scratched his head, then replied cautiously: 'Well, to tell you the truth, sir, she is and she isn't, so to speak. If we need money badly, she may take on a fellow, on occasion. But most of the time she only takes youngsters she fancies, and they get it gratis for nothing. Dead capital, that's what she is, sir! Wish she were a regular, then she'd bring in some money at least! If you'd kindly tell me, sir, how to go about getting proper papers for her, those things that say she has the right to walk the streets, and . . .'

'Only answer my questions!' Judge Dee interrupted him testily. 'Speak up, when did you begin working for Leng the pawnbroker?'

'A pawnbroker? Not me, sir! I don't deal with those bloodsuckers! My boss is Lew the Baker, of Chiang-pei.

Lives over the winehouse, near the west gate. He *was* our boss, that is. We bought ourselves out. Me, Sis and Chang.'

Judge Dee nodded. He knew that, according to the unwritten rules of the underworld, a sworn member of a gang can sever relations with his boss if he pays a certain sum of money, from which his original entrance fee, and his share in the earnings of the gang are deducted. This settling of accounts often gave rise to bitter quarrels.

'Was everything settled to the satisfaction of both parties?' he asked.

'Well, there was a bit of trouble, sir. The Baker tried to rob us, the mean son of a dog! But Uncle Twan, he was a real wizard with figures. He takes a piece of paper, does a bit of reckoning, and proves the Baker is dead wrong. The Baker didn't like that, but there were a couple of other fellows who had been following the argument, and they all said Uncle Twan was right. So the Baker had to let us go.'

'I see. Why did you want to leave the Baker's gang?'

'Because the Baker was getting too uppety, and because he was taking on jobs we didn't fancy. Jobs above our station, so to speak. The other day he wanted me and Chang to lend a hand putting two boxes across the boundary. I said no, never. First, if we get caught, we are in for big trouble. Second, the men who did those kind of big jobs for the Baker usually died in accidents afterwards. Accidents will happen, of course. But they happened too often, for my taste.'

The judge gave Tao Gan a significant look.

'When you and Chang refused, who took on the job?'

'Ying, Meng and Lau,' Seng replied promptly.

'Where are they now?'

Seng passed his thumb across his throat.

'Just accidents, mind you!' he said with a grin. But there was a glint of fear in his small eyes.

To whom were those two boxes to be delivered?' the judge asked again.

The gangster shrugged his broad shoulders.

'Heaven knows! I overheard the Baker telling Ying something about a richard who has a big store in the market-place here. I didn't ask, it wasn't my business, the less I knew about it the better. And Uncle Twan said I was dead right.'

'Where were you last night?'

'Me? I went with Sis and Chang to the Red Carp, for a bite and a little dice game. Uncle Twan said he'd eat somewhere outside, he didn't fancy dice games. When we came home at midnight, the old man hadn't come back. The poor old geezer got his head bashed in! He shouldn't have gone out alone, in a town he didn't know!'

Judge Dee took the emerald ring from his sleeve.

'Do you know this trinket?' he asked.

'Of course! That was Uncle Twan's ring. Had it from his father. "Ask him to give it to you!" I told Sis. But she said no. It's hard luck, sir, to be cursed with a sister like her!'

'Take this man back to his cell!' Judge Dee ordered the headman. 'Then tell the matron to bring Miss Seng to my office.'

While crossing the courtyard, the judge said excitedly to Tao Gan:

'You made a very nice haul! This is the first clue we've got to the smuggling case! I shall send a special messenger to my colleague in Chiang-pei at once, asking him to arrest the Baker. He will tell who his principal is, and to whom the boxes were to be delivered here. I wouldn't be astonished if that man turned out to be our friend Leng the pawnbroker! He is a wealthy man with a large store in the market-place, and he visits Chiang-pei regularly.'

'Do you think that Seng Kiu is really innocent of Twan's murder, sir? That story told by Leng's son seemed to fit him and his sister all right.'

'We shall know more about that when we have discovered the truth about that enigmatic Twan Mou-tsai, Tao Gan. I had the impression that Seng Kiu told us all he knew just now. But there must be many things that Seng does not know! We shall see what his sister has to say.'

They had entered the chancery. The senior scribe rose hurriedly and came to meet them. Handing the judge a document, he said:

'I happened to overhear Mr Tao asking our headman about a gangster called Lew the Baker, Your Honour. This routine report about the proceedings in the tribunal of Chiang-pei just came in. It contains a passage concerning that gangster.'

Judge Dee quickly glanced the paper through. With an angry exclamation he gave it to Tao Gan.

'Of all the bad luck!' he exclaimed. 'Here, read this, Tao Gan! Yesterday morning the Baker was killed in a drunken brawl!'

He walked on to his private office, angrily swinging his sleeves.

When he had sat down behind his desk he gave Tao Gan a sombre look and said dejectedly:

'I thought we were about to solve the smuggling case! And now we are back where we started. The three men who could have told us for whom the contraband was destined were murdered by the Baker. Small wonder that Ma Joong and Chiao Tai can't find them! Their bones must be rotting in a dry well, or buried under a tree in the forest! And the Baker, the only man who could have told us who the ringleaders of the smuggling are, he had to get killed!' He angrily tugged at his beard.

Tao Gan slowly wound the three long hairs that grew on

48

his cheek round his thin forefinger. After a while he said:

'Perhaps a thorough interrogation of the Baker's associates in Chiang-pei might . . .'

'No,' Judge Dee said curtly. 'The Baker killed off the men who did the dirty work for him. That he took that extreme measure proves that he was under orders from his principal to keep everything connected with the smuggling strictly secret.' He took his fan from his sleeve and began to fan himself. After a while he resumed: 'Twan's murder must be closely connected with the smuggling case. I have the distinct feeling that if we succeed in solving that crime, we shall have the key to the riddle of the smuggling ring. Come in!'

There had been a knock on the door. Now a tall, rawboned woman, clad in a simple brown robe and with a black piece of cloth wound round her head, entered the office, pushing a slender young girl in front of her.

'This is Miss Seng, Your Honour,' the matron reported in a hoarse voice.

Judge Dee gave the girl a sharp look. She stared back at him defiantly with her large, expressive eyes. Her oval, sun-tanned face was of a striking beauty. She didn't wear any make-up and she did not need it either. Her small petulant mouth was as red as a cherry, the long eyebrows above her finely chiselled nose had a natural graceful curve and the hair that hung in two tresses down to her shoulders was long and glossy. The shabby blue jacket and the patched blue trousers seemed an incongruous attire for such a beauty. She remained standing in front of the desk, her hands stuck in the straw rope round her middle that served as a belt.

After the judge had studied her for a while, he said evenly:

'We are trying to trace the whereabouts of Mr Twan Mou-tsai. Tell me where and how you met him.'

49

'If you think you'll get anything out of me, Mister Official,' she snapped, 'you are making the worst mistake of your life!'

The matron stepped forward to slap her face, but the judge raised his hand. He said calmly:

'You are standing before your magistrate, Miss Seng. You have to answer my questions, you know.'

'Think I am afraid of the whip? You can beat me as much as you like, I can stand it!'

'You won't be whipped,' Tao Gan spoke up by her side. 'Quite apart from the matter of Uncle Twan, you are guilty of vagrancy and prostitution without a licence. You'll be branded on both your cheeks.'

She suddenly grew pale.

'Don't worry!' Tao Gan added affably. 'If you put on lots of powder, the marks won't show. Not too much, at least.'

The girl stood very still, staring at the judge with scared eyes. Then she shrugged and said:

'Well, I have done nothing wrong. And I don't believe that Uncle Twan said bad things about me. Never! Where I met him? In the capital, about one year ago. I had cut my leg and walked into Twan's store to buy myself a plaster. He happened to be standing at the counter, and struck up a conversation with me, friendly like. It was the first time that such a rich fellow had shown interest in me without at once beginning to talk about you know what, and I liked him for that. I agreed to meet him that night, and so one thing led to another, if you know what I mean. He is an old man, of course, well over fifty, I'd say. But a real gentleman, nicely spoken and always ready to listen to my small talk.'

She fell silent, and looked expectantly at the judge.

'How long did the affair last?' he asked.

'A couple of weeks. Then I told Uncle Twan that we'd

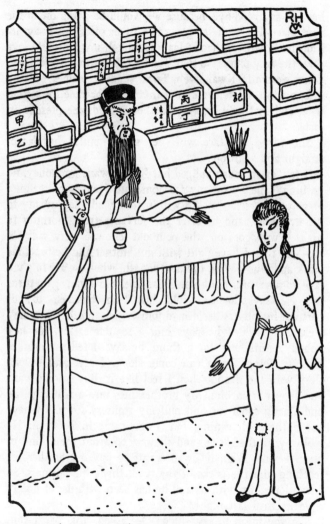

'WELL,' SHE SAID, 'I HAVE DONE NOTHING WRONG'

have to say good-bye, because we would be going on to the next place. He wants to give me a silver piece but I say no, I am not a whore, thank Heaven, though my brother'd love that, the lazy pimp! So that was that. But three weeks later, when we are in Kwang-yeh, Twan suddenly comes walking into our inn. He tells me he wants me to become his second wife, and that he'll give my brother a handsome present, in cash.'

She wiped her face with her sleeve, pulled her jacket straight and went on:

'I tell Twan much obliged but I don't want no money, no nothing. I just want my freedom, and I am not dreaming of getting myself shut up within four walls, say m'lady to his first wife, and be after the servants from morning to night. Twan goes off, the poor old fellow is very sad. Me too—for then I have fight with my brother and he beats me black and blue! Well, the next month, when we are in a village up-river, near our home Chiang-pei, old Twan again turns up. He says he has sold his drug business to his partner, for he has decided to join us. My brother says he's welcome provided he pays him a regular salary, for he's nobody's nursemaid for nothing, he says. I tell my brother nothing doing. Twan can come along, I say, and he can sleep with me if and when I feel like it. But I don't want one copper from him. My brother flies into a real rage, he and Chang catch me and pull my trousers down. I'd have got a thorough caning, but Twan came in between. He took my brother aside, and they worked out some kind of arrangement. Well, if Twan wants to pay my brother for teaching him the tricks of the road, that's his business. So Twan joined up with us and he has been with us for nearly a year. Until last night.'

'Do you mean to say,' Judge Dee asked, 'that Mr Twan, a wealthy merchant accustomed to all the luxuries of the capital, shared your life and roamed about as a common vagabond?'

'Of course he did! He liked it, I tell you. He told me a hundred times that he had never been so happy before. He said he had become fed up with life in the capital. His wives had been all right when they were young, but now they did nothing but nag, and his sons had grown up and kept interfering with his business and always wanted to teach him how he should run the store. He had been very fond of his only daughter, but she had married a merchant down south and he didn't see her any more. Also, he said, he had to attend parties every other night and that had given him a bad stomach. But after he joined us he never had any trouble with his stomach no more, he said. Besides, Chang taught him how to fish, and Uncle Twan took a powerful liking to that. Became quite good at it, too.'

The judge observed her for a while, tugging at his moustache. Then he asked:

'I suppose that Mr Twan visited many business acquaintances in the places you passed through?'

'Not him! He said he was done with all that. He only visited a colleague now and then, to get money.'

'Did Mr Twan carry large amounts of cash on his person?'

'Wrong again! About me he was silly all right, but apart from that Uncle Twan was a mighty slick business man, believe me! Never carried more than a handful of coppers on him. But every time we came to a larger city, he would go to a silver shop, and cash a draft, as he called it. Then he gave the money he received to a colleague of his, to keep for him. A wise measure, my brother being the kind of sneaky rat he is! But Uncle Twan could always get his hands on plenty of money should he need it. And when I say plenty, I mean plenty! When we came here to Han-yuan, he had five gold bars on him. Five gold bars, beg

53

your pardon! I never knew one man could have that much money all to himself! For Heaven's sake don't let my brother see that, I told Twan; he's not a killer, but for that much gold he would gladly murder the whole town! Uncle Twan smiled that little smile of his, and said he knew a safe place for putting it away. And the next day he sure enough had only one string of coppers in his pocket. Can I have a cup of tea?'

Judge Dee gave a sign to the matron. She poured the girl a cup, but her sour face clearly indicated that she disapproved of this infringement of prison rules. The judge did not notice it, for he was looking at Tao Gan. Tao Gan nodded. They were getting on the right track. After the girl had taken a few sips, Judge Dee asked:

'To whom did Mr Twan give those gold bars?'

She shrugged her shapely shoulders.

'He told me a lot about himself, but never a word about business, and I never asked him. Why should I? On our first day here, he told my brother he had to see a man who had a shop in the market-place. "I thought you had never been to Han-yuan before?" my brother asks. "I haven't," Uncle Twan says. "But I have friends!"'

'When did you see Mr Twan last?'

'Yesterday night, just before dinner. He went out and didn't come back. Had enough of it, I suppose, and went back home to the capital. That's his right, he is a free man, isn't he? But he ought to have known there was no need trying to fool me. He even went out of his way last night to tell me that he was planning to join our gang officially, so to speak, and take the oath! Why not tell me outright that we were through? I'd have missed him a bit, but not too much. A young girl like me can do without an uncle, can't she?'

'Quite. Where did he say he was going?'

'Oh, he said with that same secret smile of his that he was going to have a bite in the house of the friend he had seen our first day here. And I swallowed that!'

Judge Dee put the emerald ring on the table.

'You stated that you never accepted anything from Mr Twan. Why then did you try to pawn this ring of his?'

'I didn't! I rather liked the thing, so Uncle Twan often let me play around with it for a few days. When we happened to pass a big pawnshop the other day, I walked in to ask what it was worth, just for fun. But that fat pawnbroker tried to make up to me at once, grabbed my sleeve and whispered dirty proposals. So I walked out again.' She pushed a stray lock away from her forehead and went on with a half smile: 'It sure enough was my unlucky day! As soon as I come out, a tall bully grabs my arm and says I am his sweetheart! Gave me the creeps the way he looked at me with his bulging eyes! But Uncle Twan says at once: "Hands off, she's my girl!", and my brother he twists his arm and sends him on his way with a good kick to his behind. All men are the same, I tell you! They think you have just to lift your little finger to a vagabond girl, and hey presto she throws her arms round your neck! No, Uncle Twan was a white crow all right! And if you tell me that he has accused me of something or other, then I'll call you a liar to your face!'

Tao Gan noticed that Judge Dee did not seem to have heard her last words. Staring straight ahead, he was caressing his sidewhiskers, his thoughts apparently elsewhere. It struck Tao Gan that the judge seemed rather depressed, and he wondered what had caused this sudden change, for before the interview with Miss Seng he had been keen enough on obtaining more clues to the smuggling case. And the girl had unwittingly supplied them with valuable information. The judge too must have deduced from her rambling account that Twan had joined the gangsters only as a cover for his illegal activities; probably Twan had been the paymaster of the smuggling ring. An excellent cover, too, for who would suspect a tramp roaming the country with a couple of outlaws? And the man Twan had gone to visit in the morning must be one of the agents who distributed the contraband. A house-to-house search of all the shops in the market-place and a close interrogation of the owners would doubtless bring to light who that agent was. And through him they could find out who the ringleader was . . . the man the central authorities were so eager to discover! Tao Gan cleared his throat several times, but Judge Dee did not seem to notice it. The matron also was astonished at the prolonged silence. She darted a questioning look at Tao Gan, but the thin man could only shake his head.

The girl began to fidget. 'Stand still!' the matron snapped at her. Judge Dee looked up, startled from his musings. He pushed his cap back and told Miss Seng quietly:

'Mr Twan was murdered last night.'

'Murdered you say?' the girl burst out. 'Uncle Twan murdered? Who did it?'

'I thought you would be able to tell us,' the judge replied.

'Where was he found?' she asked tensely.

'In a deserted hut, in the forest. Half-way up the mountain slope.'

She hit her small fist on the desk and shouted with sparkling eyes:

'That bastard Lew did it! The Baker sent his men after him, because Uncle Twan had helped us to leave that rotten crowd of his! And Uncle Twan fell into the trap! The bastard, the stinking bastard!'

She buried her face in her hands and burst out in sobs.

Judge Dee waited till she had calmed down a bit. He

pointed at her cup and when she had drunk again he asked:

'Did Mr Twan, when he joined you, also cut off the tip of his left little finger?'

She smiled through her tears.

'He wanted to, but he didn't have the guts! I don't know how many times he tried, him standing with his left hand on a tree trunk and a chopper in his right, and me standing beside him and counting one two three! But he always funked it!'

The judge nodded. He thought for a few moments, then he shook his head, heaved a deep sigh and took his writing-brush. He jotted down a brief message on one of his large red visiting-cards, put it in an envelope and wrote a few words on the outside. 'Call a clerk!' he ordered Tao Gan.

When Tao Gan came back with the senior scribe, the judge gave him the envelope and said: 'Let the headman deliver this at once.' Then he turned to the girl again, gave her a thoughtful look and asked: 'Haven't you got a regular young man somewhere?'

'Yes. He's a boatman in Chiang-pei. He wants to marry me, but I told him to wait a year or two. Then he'll have a boat of his own, and I'll have had the fun I want. We'll travel up and down the canal carrying freight, making enough to keep our ricebowl filled and having a good time into the bargain!' She darted an anxious look at the judge. 'Are you really going to have my face branded, like the beanpole there said?'

'No, we won't. But you'll have to do with less freedom, for some time to come. One can have too much even of that, you know!'

He gave a sign to the matron. She took the girl's arm and led her away.

'How she rattled on!' Tao Gan exclaimed. 'It was hard to get her started, but then she went on and on without stopping!'

'I let her tell everything in her own way. A strict cross-examination is indicated only when you notice that a person is telling lies. Remember that for a subsequent occasion, Tao Gan.' He clapped his hands, and ordered the clerk who answered his summons to bring a hot towel.

'Twan Mou-tsai was a clever scoundrel, sir,' Tao Gan resumed. 'That girl is no fool, but she never understood that Twan was directing a smuggling ring.'

Judge Dee made no comment. He rearranged the papers on his desk and placed the emerald ring in the cleared space, right in front of him. The clerk brought a copper basin of hot scented water. The judge picked a towel from it, and thoroughly rubbed his face and hands. Then he leaned back in his chair and said:

'Open the window, Tao Gan. It's getting stuffy here.' He thought for a brief while, then looked up at Tao Gan and resumed: 'I don't know whether Twan was clever or not. The picture Miss Seng gave was drawn from life: an elderly man who suddenly begins to doubt the validity of all accepted standards, and wonders what he has been living for, all those years. Many men pass through this stage after they have reached a certain age. For a year or two they are a nuisance to themselves and their housemates, then they usually come round again, and laugh at their own folly. With Twan, however, it was different. He decided to make a clean break, and carried that decision to its logical conclusion, namely the starting of an entirely new life. Whether he would have regretted that decision after a few years must remain an open question. He must have been an interesting man, that Mr Twan. Eccentric, but certainly of strong character.'

The judge fell silent. Tao Gan began to shift impatiently in his chair. He was eager to discuss the next phase of the investigation. He cleared his throat a few times, then asked a bit diffidently:

'Shall we have Chang brought in for questioning now, sir?'

Judge Dee looked up.

'Chang? Oh yes, that friend of Seng Kiu, you mean. You can take care of that, Tao Gan, tomorrow. Just the routine questions. He and Seng Kiu are no problem. I was wondering about the girl, really. I don't know what to do about her! The government takes a grave view of vagrancy because it may lead to robbery and other disturbances of the peace. And also of unlicensed prostitution, because that is a form of tax evasion and therefore affects the Treasury. According to the law, she should be flogged and put in prison for two years. But I am convinced that that would turn her into a hardened criminal, who would end up either on the scaffold or in the gutter. That would be a pity, for she certainly has some sterling qualities. We must try to find another solution.'

He worriedly shook his head, and resumed:

'As to Seng Kiu and that other rascal, I'll sentence them to one year's compulsory service with the labour corps of our Northern Army. That'll cure them of their lazy habits, and give them an opportunity to show what they are worth. If they do well, they can in due course request to be enlisted as free soldiers. As regards Seng's sister . . . Yes, that's the solution, of course! I'll assign her as a bondmaid to Mr Han Yung-han! Han is a very strict, old-fashioned gentleman who keeps his large household in excellent order. If she works there for a year, she'll come to know all the advantages of a more regular life, and in due time make that young boatman of hers a good housewife!'

Tao Gan gave the judge a worried look. He thought he really seemed very tired, his face was pale and the lines beside his mouth had become more marked. It had indeed been a long day. Would the judge consider it presumptuous if he proposed to take charge of the routine check of the shops in the market-place? Or let him question Leng again? He decided first to ascertain what Judge Dee's own plans were.

'What do you think should be our next step now, sir? I thought . . .'

'Our next step?' the judge asked raising his tufted eyebrows. 'There is no next step. Didn't you see that all our problems are solved? Now we know how and why Twan was murdered, who took his dead body to the hut, everything! Including, of course, who was acting as local agent for the smuggling ring.' As Tao Gan stared at him, dumbfounded, the judge went on impatiently: 'Heavens, you have heard all the evidence, haven't you? If I am now winding up with you the side-issues it's only because I have nothing better to do while I am waiting for the central figure of this tragedy to make his appearance.'

Tao Gan opened his mouth to speak but Judge Dee went on quickly:

'Yes, it is indeed a tragedy. Often, Tao Gan, the final solution of a complicated case gives me a feeling of satisfaction, the satisfaction of having righted a wrong, and solved a riddle. This, however, is a case that depresses me. Strange, I had a vague foreboding of it when I had this ring here in my hand early this morning, just after I had got it from the gibbon. This ring emanated an atmosphere of human suffering. . . . Suffering is a terrible thing, Tao Gan. Sometimes it dignifies, mostly it degrades. Presently we shall see how it affected the main actor in this drama, and . . .'

He broke off his sentence and glanced at the door. Footsteps had sounded in the corridor outside. The headman ushered in Mr Wang.

The pharmacist, small and dapper in his glossy robe of black silk, made a low bow.

'What can this person do for Your Honour?' he asked politely.

Judge Dee pointed at the emerald ring before him and said evenly:

'You may tell me why you didn't take this ring too when you removed the dead man's possessions.'

Wang gave a violent start when he saw the ring. But he quickly mastered himself and said indignantly:

'I don't understand this at all, Your Honour! The headman brought me your visiting-card with the request to come here to give some information, and . . .'

'Yes,' the judge interrupted him. 'Information about the murder of your colleague Twan Mou-tsai!' The pharmacist wanted to speak but Judge Dee raised his hand. 'No, listen to me! I know exactly what happened. You badly needed the five gold bars Mr Twan had entrusted to you, for your plan to smuggle two boxes of valuable contraband from Chiang-pei into Han-yuan had miscarried. The Baker's men whom you had hired bungled it, and the military police seized the costly merchandise you probably hadn't even paid for. Twan's desire to join Miss Seng's gang by taking the formal oath and cutting off the tip of his left little finger gave you an excellent opportunity for murdering that unfortunate man.'

The headman moved up close to Wang, but Judge Dee shook his head at him. He continued:

'Twan lacked the courage to cut off the fingertip himself, and you had promised to perform the operation for him last night, in your own house up on the ridge. You had agreed that it would be done with the large chopper used for cut-

61

ting medicinal roots into thin slices. One end of the heavy, razor-edged knife is attached with a hinge to the cutting board, the handle is on the other end. By means of this precision-instrument, which every pharmacist and drug-dealer has at hand, the operation could be performed without the risk of cutting off too much or too little, and so quickly and smoothly that the pain would be reduced to a minimum. Twan went to all this trouble because he wanted to prove to the vagabond girl he loved that he intended to stay with her forever.'

The judge paused. Wang stared at him with wide, unbelieving eyes.

'Before Twan had even placed his hand in the right position on the cutting board, the large chopper came down and cut off four of his fingers. Then the unfortunate old man was finished off by bashing in his skull with the iron pestle of a drug mortar. Afterwards his dead body was carried from your house downhill to the deserted hut. There it would have been discovered, probably after many weeks, in an advanced state of decay. Moreover, you had taken the precaution of searching the body and removing everything that could have given a clue to the dead man's identity. I would have had the corpse burned as that of an unidentified tramp. But a gibbon of the forest put me on the right track.'

'A ... a gibbon?' Wang stammered.

'Yes, the gibbon who found Twan's emerald ring, which I have here before me. But that is no concern of yours.'

Judge Dee fell silent. It was completely quiet in the small office.

Wang's face had turned ashen and his lips were twitching. He swallowed a few times before he spoke, in a voice so hoarse that it was hardly audible:

'Yes, I confess that I murdered Twan Mou-tsai. Everything happened exactly as you said. With the exception of your remark about the two boxes of contraband. Those were not my property, I was acting only as an agent, I was to have redistributed their contents.' He sighed and continued in a detached voice: 'I have had a number of financial reverses, these last two years, and my creditors were pressing me. The man whom I was most indebted to was a banker, in the capital.' He mentioned a name which Judge Dee recognized; the man was a well-known financier, a cousin of the Director of the Treasury. 'He wrote me a letter saying that, if I would come to see him, he was willing to talk matters over. I travelled to the capital and he received me most kindly. He said that, if I agreed to collaborate with him on a certain financial scheme of his, he would not only cancel my bonds, but also give me a generous share in the proceeds. Of course I agreed. Then, to my horrified amazement, he went on to explain coolly that he had organized a nation-wide smuggling ring!'

Wang passed his hand over his eyes. Shaking his head, he resumed:

'When he mentioned the enormous profits, I weakened. Finally I gave in. I . . . I can't afford to become a poor man. And when I thought of all that money I would receive . . . I should have known better! Instead of cancelling my bonds, the cruel devil held on to them, and his idea of rewarding me for my services was to lend me money at an atrocious interest. Soon I was completely in his clutches. When Twan entrusted the five gold bars to me, I thought at once that this was my chance to pay my principal, and become a free man again. I knew that Twan had told nobody that he would come to my house last night, for he didn't want others to know that he lacked the courage to perform the operation himself. He had insisted that I wouldn't even tell my family of his impending visit. I myself let him in, by the back door.'

The pharmacist took a silk handkerchief from his sleeve and wiped his moist face. Then he said firmly:

'If Your Honour will kindly let me have a sheet of paper, I shall now write out my formal confession that I wilfully murdered Twan Mou-tsai.'

'I haven't asked you for a formal confession yet, Mr Wang,' Judge Dee said calmly. 'There are a few points that have to be clarified. In the first place: why did Mr Twan want to have such large sums of money always at his disposal?'

'Because he kept hoping that some day that vagabond girl would consent to marry him. He told me that he wanted to be able to pay off her brother at once, and buy a nice country seat somewhere, to start a new life.'

'I see. Second: why didn't you tell Twan frankly that you needed his gold because you were in serious financial trouble? Isn't it the old-established custom that members of the same guild always assist each other? And Mr Twan was a very wealthy man who could well afford to lend you five gold bars.'

Wang seemed greatly upset by these questions. His lips moved, but he could not bring out a word. Judge Dee did not pursue the matter further and went on:

'Third, you are a slightly-built elderly man. How did you manage to carry the corpse all the way to the hut? It's true that it is downhill, but even so I don't think you could have done it.'

Wang had taken hold of himself. Shaking his head disconsolately he answered:

'I can't understand myself how I did it, sir! But I was frantic, obsessed by the idea that I had to hide the body, at once. That gave me the force to drag the corpse to the garden, and from there to the forest. When I came back to the house, I was more dead than alive. . . .' Again he mopped his face. Then he added in a firmer voice: 'I fully realize that I have murdered a good man because of his money, sir, and that I shall have to pay for that crime with my life.'

Judge Dee sat up straight. Placing his elbows on the desk he leaned forward and told Wang in a gentle voice:

'You didn't realize, however, that if you formally confess to this murder, all your possessions will be confiscated, Mr Wang. Besides, your son wouldn't inherit in any case, for I shall have to have him certified as of unsound mind.'

'What do you mean?' Wang shouted. He bent forward and crashed his fist on the desk. 'It isn't true, it's a lie! My son is very sound of mind, I tell you! The boy's mental development is only a bit retarded, and he's only twenty, after all! When he grows older, his mind will doubtless improve. . . . With a little patience, and if one avoids getting him excited, he is perfectly normal!'

He gave the judge an imploring look and went on with a shaking voice:

'He is my only son, sir, and such a nice, obedient boy! I assure you, sir . . .'

Judge Dee spoke quietly:

'I shall personally see to it that he is given every possible care, Mr Wang, during your term in prison. I give you my word for that. But if we don't take adequate measures, your son will cause more accidents. He must be placed in ward, that's the only solution. Two days ago, when he came out of your shop, he happened to see that vagabond girl who was just leaving Leng's pawnshop. She is very beautiful, and in his confused mind your son thought she was his sweetheart. He wanted to take hold of her, but Mr Twan told him she was *his* sweetheart, and then Miss Seng's brother chased your son away. This occurrence made a deep impression on his poor, deranged mind. Yesterday, when

65

Twan came to visit you, your son must have seen him. Convinced that this was the man who had stolen his sweetheart from him, he killed him. Then you let your son carry the corpse to the hut, you leading the way. For your son that was an easy job, for like many young men of unsound mind, he is exceptionally strong and tall.'

Wang nodded dazedly. Deep lines marked his pale, drawn face, his shoulders were sagging. He had suddenly changed from a dapper, efficient merchant into a tired old man.

'So that is why he kept talking about the girl and Twan. . . . I was taken completely unawares last night, for the boy had been in such a good mood, the whole day. . . . In the afternoon I had taken him for a walk in the woods, and he was so happy, watching the gibbons in the trees. . . . He dined with the housemaster, then he went to bed, for he tires easily. . . . I had told the housemaster that I would dine alone, in my library, had him put a cold snack there ready for me. When I was eating there with Twan, I told him about the gold. He said at once that I needn't worry about that, he could easily order more from the capital should he need it, and I could pay him back in instalments. "The kind help you shall extend to me presently," he added with a smile, "I shall consider as the interest on the loan!" Twan was like that, sir. A truly remarkable man. He quickly emptied a large beaker of wine, then we went to the small workshop I have in my garden shed, to experiment with new drugs. Twan put his left hand on the cutting board, and closed his eyes. Just when I was adjusting the chopper, someone gave a push against my elbow. "The bad old man has stolen my girl!" my son cried out behind me. The chopper had clapped down and cut off four fingers of Twan's hand. He fell forward over the table, with a frightened cry. I quickly looked round for a jar of powder, to staunch the bleeding. Suddenly my son grabbed an iron pestle from

66

the table and hit him a terrible blow on the back of his head. . . .'

He gave the judge a forlorn look. Then, grabbing the edge of the desk with both hands, he said:

'The bright moon shining into his bedroom had wakened the boy, and looking out of his window he had seen Twan and me going to the garden shed. The moonlight always brings him into a kind of trance. . . . My boy didn't know what he did, Your Honour! He is so gentle as a rule, he . . .' His voice trailed off.

'Your son shan't be prosecuted, of course, Mr Wang. Mentally deficient persons are outside the pale of the law. Mr Tao here will now take you to his own office next door, and there you will draw up a document describing to the best of your knowledge the organization and activities of the smuggling ring, adding the names and addresses of all other agents known to you. Is Mr Leng, the pawnbroker, among them, by the way?'

'Oh no, sir! Why should you suspect him? He is my neighbour, and I never . . .'

'I was told that he regularly visits Chiang-pei, one of the important bases of your smuggling organization.'

'Mr Leng's wife is extremely jealous,' Wang remarked dryly. 'She doesn't allow him to have other women in the house. Therefore he established a separate household in Chiang-pei.'

'Quite. Well, after you have signed and sealed the document I mentioned, Mr Wang, you will then write a complete account of Mr Twan's fatal accident. This very night I shall send both documents by special messenger to the capital. I shall add a recommendation for clemency, pointing out that you voluntarily furnished the information that will enable the authorities to break up the smuggling ring. I hope this will result in your prison term being substantially reduced. However that may be, I shall try to arrange that your son is allowed to visit you from time to time in prison. Take Mr Wang to your room, Tao Gan. Supply him with writing material, and give strict orders that he is not to be disturbed.'

When Tao Gan came back, he found Judge Dee standing in front of the open window, his hands behind his back. He was enjoying the cool air that came inside from the small walled-in garden, planted with banana trees. Pointing at the mass of luxuriant green leaves he said:

'Look at those magnificent bunches of bananas, Tao Gan! They have just ripened. Tell the headman to bring a few to my private residence, so that I can give the gibbons some, tomorrow morning.'

Tao Gan nodded, his long face creased in a broad smile.

'Allow me to congratulate you, sir, on . . .'

Judge Dee raised his hand.

'It was thanks to your prompt and efficient action that we could solve this complicated case so quickly, Tao Gan. I apologize for being rather curt with you, just before Mr Wang came in. The fact is that I was dreading that interview, for I hate nothing more than to see a man go all to pieces in front of me—even if he is a criminal. But Mr Wang bore himself well. His great love for his son lent him dignity, Tao Gan.'

The judge resumed his seat behind the desk.

'I shall write a letter to Sergeant Hoong in Chiang-pei at once, informing him that the smuggling case has been solved, and that he and my other two lieutenants must come back here tomorrow. And you can issue the necessary orders for the release from prison of our friend the pawnbroker. Those hours in jail will have given him an opportunity for reflection, I hope.'

He took up his writing-brush, but suddenly he checked himself and resumed:

'Now that I have worked together closely with you alone on a case, Tao Gan, I want to tell you that I shall be very glad to have you on my permanent staff. I have but one piece of advice to give to you for your further career as a criminal investigator. That is that you must never allow yourself to become emotionally involved in the cases you are dealing with. This is most important, Tao Gan, but most difficult to achieve. I ought to know. I have never learned it.'

THE NIGHT OF THE TIGER

THE NIGHT OF THE TIGER

Huddled up in his heavy fur coat, the judge was riding all alone along the highway across the deserted plain. It was late in the afternoon, the grey shadows of the winter night were hovering already over the bleak, flooded land, through which the raised highway cut like a crack in a tarnished mirror. The water reflected the leaden sky that seemed to hang very low over the rippling waves. The north wind drove masses of dark rain-clouds towards the mist-covered mountains in the distance.

Deep in thought, the judge had ridden ahead, leaving the armed men of his escort more than half a mile behind. Hunched over the neck of his horse, his fur cap pulled well down over his ears, he stared straight at the road before him. He was aware that his thoughts ought to dwell on the future. In two days' time he would be in the imperial capital and assuming his new post, the high office he had been appointed to quite unexpectedly. But constantly his mind went back to the past week. The tragic experience that had marked his last days as magistrate of Pei-chow kept nagging at him, dragging him back to that small, dismal district high up in the frozen north which they had left three days before.*

For three days they had been riding south through the snow-bound northern country. Then a sudden thaw had set in. It was causing disastrous floods in the province they had entered now. In the morning they had met long files of

* See *The Chinese Nail Murders*, London, Michael Joseph, 1961.

peasants, fleeing north from their inundated fields, wearily trudging along bent under the bundles of their scanty belongings, their feet wrapped in mud-covered rags. When they had halted for the noon-rice at the traffic control station, the captain commanding the judge's escort had reported that they were coming now to the worst stretch, where the Yellow River had overflown its entire north bank; he had advised waiting there for more information on the water-level in the area ahead. But the judge had decided that they would travel on, for he was under orders to proceed to the capital without delay. Besides, he knew from the map that across the river the land rose, and there stood the fortress where he planned to stay the night.

The highway was completely deserted. A few isolated roofs of submerged farmsteads sticking up here and there from the mass of muddy water were the only signs that this had been until recently a fertile, well-populated plain. When the judge came nearer to the mountain range, however, he saw two barracks on the left side of the road ahead. About a dozen men were standing there, close together. As he rode up to them he saw that they were local militia, wearing thick leather caps and jackets and knee-high boots. A stretch of the highway had crumbled away there, leaving a gap of more than a hundred feet through which rushed a stream of turbid water. The men were worriedly looking at the low wall of faggots that reinforced the sides of their improvised bridgehead.

A narrow temporary bridge led across the gap to the opposite bank, where the highway went up the thickly wooded mountain slope. The bridge had been hastily constructed from heavy logs, lashed together with thick hempropes. It rose and fell with the churning water it was half floating on.

'It isn't safe to cross, sir!' the leader of the militia called out. 'The current is growing stronger all the time, and we can't keep the bridge clear. Better turn back. If the ropes break, we'll have to abandon this bridgehead.'

The judge turned round in his saddle. Narrowing his eyes against the biting north wind, he peered at the group of horsemen in the distance. They were riding at a fast pace, he thought they would catch up with him soon. After a glance at the hills over on the other side of the gap, he decided to take the chance. According to the roadmap, it was only half an hour's ride across the mountain range to the Yellow River. There the ferry would carry him to the fortress on the south bank.

He drove his horse onto the slippery logs. The bridge swayed to and fro, and the thick ropes creaked as he advanced cautiously, his horse stepping ahead with stiff legs. When he was about half-way, muddy waves came lapping over the logs. He patted the neck of his horse reassuringly. Suddenly a tree trunk, carried along by the current, crashed against the bridge. The billows that came surging over the logs rose up to the belly of his horse and thoroughly wet his riding boots. The judge urged the prancing animal ahead, onto the second half of the bridge. There the logs were dry, and soon they were on firm ground again. He made his horse step quickly up the high bank, then halted under the tall trees. Just as he turned his head round there was a loud crashing sound. Now a large cluster of uprooted trees had smashed into the bridge. Its central section heaved upwards like the curving back of a dragon, then the ropes tore and the logs came apart. There was nothing left between him and the bridgehead but a mass of foaming water.

He waved his riding-whip at the militia to signify that he was riding on. His escort would come along as soon as the bridge had been repaired. He would wait for them in the fortress.

After the first bend he was under the lee of the dark, tall

oak trees that rose on either side of the road. Now he realized, however, how cold his feet were in their soggy boots. But it was a relief to be on firm ground again after the long ride through the flooded region.

Suddenly there was the sound of breaking branches. A wild-looking horseman came out from the thick undergrowth. His long hair was bound up with a piece of red cloth, a short cape of tigerskin hung round his wide shoulders and a broadsword was dangling on his back. He brought his horse to a halt in the middle of the road, thus barring the way. Fixing the judge with his small, cruel eyes, he let his short spear whirl around by a quick, two-handed movement.

The judge halted his horse.

'Get out of my way!' he shouted.

The other let go of the tip of the spear, holding on to the butt end. The sharp point described a wide circle, grazing the forelock of Judge Dee's horse. As the judge pulled the reins, all the pent-up emotions of the last few days found an outlet in a sudden, savage rage. He raised his hand to his right shoulder and, quick as lightning, drew the sword hanging on his back. He aimed a long blow at the bandit, but the ruffian parried it expertly with the point of his spear, and at once tried to hit Judge Dee's head with the butt end. The judge ducked, but then the spear point came whirling down on him. He caught the shaft on the razor-sharp edge of his sword, and the wood was cut clean through. As the robber was looking, amazed, at the stump in his hand, the judge pressed his horse on close to the other, and raised his sword for the death blow on the other's neck. But the man swung his horse round with his knees practically at the same time, and the sword swished over his head. The ruffian uttered a vile curse but made no move to draw his sword. He urged his horse on to the farther side of the road and shouted over his shoulder:

JUDGE DEE CAUGHT THE SPEAR ON HIS SWORD

'One more rat in the trap!'

He grinned, then disappeared into the thick foliage.

The judge sheathed his sword. Driving on his horse, he reflected that he must pull himself together. An insolent highwayman ought not to be sufficient cause for losing his temper. The impact of the tragedy at Pei-chow had affected him deeply, so deeply that he wondered forlornly whether he would ever succeed in regaining his inward peace.

He met no one while ascending the last ridge, and when he had arrived on the top he caught again the full blast of the north wind. Penetrating his thick fur coat, it chilled him to the bone. He quickly rode down to the bank and halted his horse in front of the vast expanse of the swollen river. Its churning waves beat against the rocky shore farther to the west. The opposite bank was shrouded in a low-hanging mist. There was no sign of a ferry, and of the quay only two broken pillars were left. White foam spurted up against them. The waves rushed on from east to west with a low rumbling sound, carrying along heavy logs and clusters of green shrubs.

With a frown the judge surveyed the desolate scene, dismal and grey in the gathering dusk. The only habitation in sight was a large old country house, standing all by itself on a low hill a mile or so to the west. It was surrounded by a high wall; on the east corner stood a watchtower. The whiffs of smoke rising up from the roof of the main building were carried away swiftly by the strong wind.

Stifling a sigh the judge guided his horse to the winding road that led up to the hill. He had come to a dead end. It couldn't be helped, he and his retinue would have to break their journey here, pending the repair of the ferry.

The ground surrounding the country house was covered by tall grass and large boulders. There were no trees, but the mountain slope behind it was thickly wooded. Some people were moving about there, in front of what seemed to be the mouth of a large cave. Three horsemen came from among the trees and rode down the mountain slope.

When the judge was about half-way to the house, his eye fell on a high stake driven into the ground by the roadside. A bulky object hung from its top. Bending over in the saddle, he saw that it was the severed head of a man. The long hair fluttered across the distorted face. A pair of cut-off hands was nailed to the stake, directly below the head. Shaking his head perplexedly, the judge pressed his horse on.

As he arrived in front of the high gatehouse with its solid, iron-bound double door, it struck him that the place looked like a small fort rather than a country house. The high crenelated walls sloping down to a broad base seemed unusually heavy, and there was not a single window in sight.

Just when he was about to knock on the gate with the butt of his riding-whip, it swung open slowly. An old peasant motioned him to enter a spacious, semi-dark yard, paved with cobblestones, and as the judge jumped down from his horse, he heard the grating sound of the cross-bar of the gate being pushed back into its place.

A gaunt man in a long blue gown and a small skull-cap on his head came rushing towards him. Thrusting his lean face close to that of the judge he panted:

'Saw you from the watchtower! Shouted at once at the gatekeeper to open up. Glad they didn't overtake you!'

He had an intelligent face, adorned by a ragged moustache and a short goatee. The judge put him in his early forties. The man took a quick look at Judge Dee's bedraggled appearance, and resumed:

'You have a long journey behind you, evidently! My name is Liao, by the way. I am the steward here, you see.' Now that he had regained his breath, he spoke with a pleasant voice. He seemed a well-educated gentleman.

'My name is Dee. I am a magistrate from up north, on my way to the capital.'

'Good Heavens, a magistrate! I must inform Mr Min. At once!'

The gaunt man ran to the main building in the rear of the yard, agitatedly swinging his arms. The flapping sleeves reminded the judge of a frightened chicken. He now became conscious of a low murmur of voices. It came from the outhouses to the left and right of the courtyard. A few dozen men and women were squatting under the eaves and among the pillars there. Behind them stood piles of large bundles, wrapped in blue cloth and fastened by thick straw ropes. By the nearest pillar sat a peasant woman suckling a small child, half covered by her ragged cloak. Over the low wall came the neighing of horses. He thought he had better take his horse there, for it was wet and tired. When he led it to the narrow doorway in the corner, the murmur of voices ceased abruptly.

The walled-in enclosure proved to be indeed the stable yard. Half a dozen grown-up boys were busying themselves there about a few large, brightly-coloured kites. One of them looked up excitedly at the red kite that flew high in the grey sky, its long string taut in the strong wind. Judge Dee asked the tallest boy to rub down and feed his horse. He patted its neck, then walked back to the courtyard.

A short, portly gentleman wearing a thick robe of grey wool and a flat cap of the same material came rushing down the broad steps of the three-storied main building.

'How did you get through, magistrate?' he asked, excitedly.

Judge Dee raised his eyebrows at the abrupt question.

'On my horse,' he replied curtly.

'But what about the Flying Tigers?'

'I met no tigers, flying or otherwise. Would you kindly explain what you . . .'

The judge broke off in mid-sentence as a tall, broad-shouldered man, dressed in a long fur coat, brushed past the portly gentleman. He set his square cap right and asked politely:

'Are you travelling all alone, sir?'

'No, I have sixty soldiers with me. They . . .'

'Heaven be praised!' the fat man exclaimed. 'We are saved!'

'Where are they?' the tall man asked eagerly.

'At the bridgehead, on the other side of the mountain range. The bridge over the gap there broke down just after I had crossed it. My men will be here as soon as it has been repaired.'

The fat man threw up his arms in despair.

'Ever seen such a fool?' he asked his companion angrily.

'Look here, you!' the judge snapped. 'You shan't call me names! Are you the master of this house? I want shelter for the night.'

'Shelter? Here?' the other scoffed.

'Calm yourself, Mr Min!' the tall man said sharply. And, to the judge: 'I hope you'll excuse our bad manners, sir. But we are in a most awful predicament. This gentleman is Mr Min Kwo-tai, the younger brother of the landowner, who is gravely ill. Mr Min came here yesterday, to be on hand if his brother's illness should take a turn for the worse. I am Yen Yuan, the bailiff of the Min estate. Shall we take our guest inside, Mr Min?'

Without waiting for the other's assent, he led Judge Dee up the stone steps. They entered a cavernous, windowless hall, lit by a huge open fire that blazed up in a square hole in the centre of the bare, stoneflagged floor. It was sparsely furnished with a few large, well-worn pieces: two broad

81

black-wood cupboards and a high-backed bench against the side wall, and a thick-legged table of carved ebony in the rear. These solid antique pieces went well with the heavy, smoke-blackened rafters of the low ceiling. The plastered walls were bare. Evidently the arrangements of the hall had not been interfered with for a great many years. There was the comfortable atmosphere of rustic simplicity, typical of the old-style country house.

While crossing the hall to the table at the back, the judge noticed that the house was built on two different levels: on either side a few steps led up to small side-rooms, separated from the hall by partition screens of open lattice work. Through the screen on the left the judge saw a high desk, piled with account books. It was apparently the office.

The bailiff lit the candlestick on the table, then offered the judge the capacious armchair behind it. He himself took the chair on the left. Mr Min, who had been muttering to himself all the time, sank down in the smaller armchair on the opposite side. While the bailiff busied himself about the tea tray, Judge Dee unfastened his sword and laid it on the small wall table. He loosened his fur coat and sat down. Leaning back in his chair, he covertly observed the two men, slowly caressing his long sidewhiskers.

Yen Yuan, the bailiff, was not difficult to place. His handsome, regular face with the jet-black moustache and the neatly trimmed chinbeard, together with his slightly affected accent, indicated the young man about town. Although he could not be much older than twenty-five, there were dark pouches under his heavy-lidded eyes, and deep lines by the side of his loose, rather sensual mouth. The judge wondered idly how a typical gay young blade from the city came to be bailiff on an isolated country estate. When Yen had placed a large tea cup of coarse green earthenware before him, the judge asked casually:

'Are you related to the landowner, Mr Yen?'

'To the old mistress, rather, sir. My parents live in the provincial capital. My father sent me here last year, for a change of air. I have been rather ill.'

'Soon we'll be cured of all our ills. For good!' the fat man muttered crossly.

He spoke with a broad country brogue; but his heavy-jowled, haughty face, framed by grey whiskers and a long, straggling beard, seemed to point to a businessman from the city.

'What illness is your brother suffering from, Mr Min?' the judge inquired politely.

'Asthma, aggravated by a heart condition,' Mr Min replied curtly. 'Might live to be a hundred, if he took proper care of himself. The doctors told him to take it easy, for a year or so. But no, he would gad about in the fields, rain or shine! So I had to come rushing out here. Had to leave my tea firm to my assistant, that lazy good-for-nothing! What will become of my business, of my family, I ask you? Those blasted Flying Tigers will put us to the sword, every one of us. Confounded bad luck!'

He set his tea cup down on the table hard, and angrily combed his beard with the short fingers of his podgy hand.

'I presume,' Judge Dee said, 'that you are referring to a band of highwaymen that is infesting this area. For I was waylaid by an armed robber on the road, who wore a cape of tigerskin. He didn't put up much of a fight, though. Well, unfortunately severe floods often tempt vagabonds and other riff-raff to profit from the disrupted traffic and the general confusion and engage in assault and robbery. But you need not worry, Mr Min. My military escort is armed to the teeth, so that those robbers would never dare to raid this country house. My men will be here as soon as the bridge has been repaired.'

'Almighty Heaven!' Mr Min shouted at the bailiff. 'When the bridge is repaired, he says! That's officials for you!' Taking hold of himself with an effort, he asked the judge in a calmer voice:

'Where do you suppose the timber would come from, worthy sir? There isn't a stick of timber to be had for miles around!'

'You are talking nonsense!' the judge said testily. 'What about the oak forest I just passed through?'

The fat man glared at the judge, then he sat back in his chair and asked the bailiff with a resigned air: 'Would you be kind enough to explain the situation, Mr Yen?'

The bailiff took a chopstick from the tea tray. Having laid it on the table in front of the judge, he placed an inverted tea cup on either side of it.

'This chopstick is the Yellow River,' he began. 'It flows here from east to west. This tea cup on the south bank is the fort, the cup on the opposite bank represents this country house.' He dipped his forefinger in the tea, and drew an oval round the latter cup. 'This is the mountain range here, the only tract of elevated ground this side of the river. All the rest of the surrounding country consists of rice fields; they belong to the landowner here, for about six miles north. Well, the river rose till it overflowed the south bank, transforming this mountain range into an island. A section of the raised highway north of the range crumbled away, as you saw when you crossed the temporary bridge the militia built over the gap. The ferry on this side was carried away by the current yesterday afternoon; Mr Min and a party of travelling merchants were the last to use it, yesterday morning. This country house is the only inhabited place hereabouts. So, you see that we are completely isolated, sir. Heaven only knows when the ferry can be re-installed, and it will take days before they have brought down from up north the

84

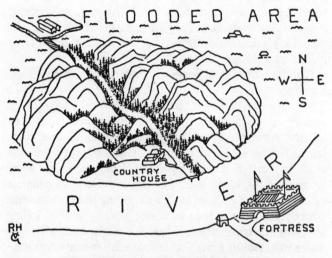

SKETCHMAP OF THE FLOODED AREA

timber necessary for repairing the bridge over the gap. There isn't a single tree for miles around north of the gap, as you must have seen for yourself when you came riding south.'

Judge Dee nodded.

'I see that you have a number of refugees here, however,' he remarked. 'Why not select a dozen sturdy peasants from among them, and send them on horseback to the gap? They could fell trees, and . . .'

'Didn't you see the severed head on the stake by the road-side when you came up here?' Mr Min interrupted.

'I did. What does that mean?'

'It means,' the portly gentleman replied in a surly voice, 'that those bandits keep a careful watch on us—from their caves up the mountain slope, behind the house here. The head you saw is that of our groom. We had sent him to the

85

gap, to inform the militia of our predicament. Well, just when he was about to take the highway, six horsemen swooped down on him. They dragged him back here, first cut off his hands and feet, then beheaded him, right in front of our gatehouse.'

'The insolent dogs!' Judge Dee called out angrily. 'How many are they?'

'About a hundred, sir,' the bailiff answered. 'All of them heavily armed, seasoned fighters, and desperate men. They are the remnants of a strong robber band of over three hundred who infested the lonely mountain region in the southern part of the province half a year ago. The army drove them away, but then they began to roam the country-side, burning the farmsteads and killing the inhabitants. Army patrols chased them from one place to another, killing about two-thirds of them. They fled north, and, when the water rose, sought refuge on this deserted mountain range.

'They established themselves in the caves, and posted look-outs on the top of the range, and down at the gap. They had planned to lie low here till the water fell, but when the ferry was carried away, and they did not need to be afraid any longer of being attacked by the soldiers from the fort, they conceived a better plan. Yesterday six of them came to the gate here. They asked for two hundred gold pieces; travel-ling funds, as they chose to call it. They would leave the next morning, they said, on the rafts a few of them are building on the west point of the island. If we refused to pay, they would storm this country house, and put every-one inside to the sword. They must have had a spy among our servants, for the sum they asked for represents just about the amount of cash the landowner usually keeps in his strongbox.'

The bailiff shook his head, cleared his throat and went on: 'My master decided to pay. The bandits said their leader would come personally to fetch the gold. Mr Min and I went to my master's room, he gave us the key, and we opened the strongbox. It was empty. The gold had been stolen. Since one of the maidservants absconded that same night, we suspect that it was she who stole the gold.

'When we told the leader of the Flying Tigers that the gold was gone, he flew into an awful rage. He accused us of trying to gain time by base trickery, and said that if the gold was not brought to his cave before nightfall today, he would come down with his men to take it himself, and kill all of us. In despair we sent out the groom to contact the militia at the gap. And you have just heard what they did to him.'

'To think that the fortress is just across the river!' the judge muttered. 'They have more than a thousand soldiers there!'

'Not to speak of several hundred heavily armed river police, who congregated there when they had to evacuate the traffic control stations up river,' Yen remarked. 'But how can we establish contact with the fortress?'

'What about a signal fire?' the judge asked. 'If the men in the fortress saw that, they . . .'

'They wouldn't come even if this whole house was afire,' Mr Min said, glaring angrily at the judge.

'That's true, sir,' the bailiff said quickly. 'A large war-junk could eventually get across the swollen river, but it would be a major undertaking, and not without risk. First they would have to tug the empty junk for a good distance up river. After the soldiers had gone on board it would then have to be rowed across in a slow curve, and beached in a suitable place on the bank down here—an operation calling for very superior navigation. The commandant of the fort would risk it, of course, if he knew that the notorious Flying Tigers are marooned here—a Heaven-sent chance for exterminating that band of outlaws once and for all. The bandits realize that, of course; that's why they keep quiet. When the ferry was still being operated, they let a group of merchants going south pass unmolested.'

'I must admit,' the judge said, nodding slowly, 'that the situation is far from cheerful, to say the least.'

'I am glad you see that now, magistrate,' Mr Min remarked sourly.

'However,' Judge Dee resumed, 'this country house is built like a small fortress. If you issued arms to the refugees, we could . . .'

'Of course we too have thought of that,' Mr Min interrupted. 'Want a list of the arms at our disposal? Two rusty spears, four hunting bows with a dozen arrows, and three swords. I beg you pardon, four swords, counting yours on the wall table there.'

'Until about a hundred years ago,' the bailiff said, 'our family kept a well-stocked armoury here, and they maintained twenty or so braves on the premises, as a permanent bodyguard. But all those costly precautionary measures were of course dropped after the fortress had been built. So you see, magistrate, that . . .'

He looked round. The gaunt steward was coming up to their table with his long stride.

'I told the gatekeeper to take over from me in the watch-tower, sir,' he addressed Mr Min respectfully. 'The cook came to tell me that the rice gruel for the refugees is ready.'

'Forty-six extra mouths to fill,' Mr Min informed the judge gloomily. 'I counted them myself, man, woman and child.' He heaved a deep sigh and added in a resigned voice: 'All right, let's go.'

'Shouldn't we show the magistrate a room first, sir?' the bailiff asked. 'He'll be eager to change.'

Mr Min hesitated for one brief moment before he replied, curtly:

'My brother will have to decide that. He is the master here.' Turning to the judge, he went on: 'If you'll excuse us for a while, sir, I'll have to attend to the feeding of the refugees, with Yen and Liao. All the servants here fled when they heard about the arrival of the bandits, you see. We have only the gatekeeper, and the old couple I brought with me from the city. So you'll understand that we can't offer you the hospitality your rank entitles you to, and . . .'

'Of course!' the judge interrupted hastily. 'Don't bother about me! I shall sleep on that bench down there against the wall, and I . . .'

'My brother shall decide,' Mr Min repeated firmly. He rose and left the hall, followed by Yen and the steward.

Judge Dee poured himself another cup of tea. Upon his arrival he had said he was a magistrate, so as not to embarrass his unseen host; even the biggest landowner would have been at a loss how to entertain properly a metropolitan official of his present high rank. Now that he had learned the awkward situation here, he was all the more glad that he had not revealed his true status.

He emptied his cup, got up and walked to the door. Standing at the head of the steps, he looked out at the yard, which was now lit by a number of smoking torches. The bailiff and the steward stood by a huge iron cauldron, busily ladling the gruel into the bowls of the people filing past. Mr Min was supervising them, from time to time gruffly warning the peasants not to push one another. Half of them were women and children, some of the latter mere infants. It would never do to let these people fall into the hands of the bandits. The Flying Tigers would slay the men, elderly women and infants on the spot, and take the young boys and girls away to be sold as slaves. He had to do something. Angrily tugging at his beard, he reflected bitterly how relative worldly power was. He, the Lord Chief Justice of the Empire, and President of the Metropolitan Court, had, through the force of circumstances, suddenly been reduced to a helpless traveller!

He turned on his heels and crossed the hall to the small office on the left. After he had seated himself in the capacious armchair, he folded his arms in his wide sleeves and looked up at the faded landscape painting that decorated the wall opposite. It was flanked by two long and narrow scrolls, inscribed with classical quotations, in bold, original calligraphy. The one on the right read:

Above, the Sovereign rules the realm,
   in accordance with the Mandate of Heaven.

The other one bore the parallel line:

Below, the peasants are the foundation of the State,
   they till the land in accordance with the seasons.

Judge Dee nodded approvingly. He remained sitting there for some time, staring straight ahead. Suddenly he sat up, took his hands from his sleeves and pulled the candle closer. He tilted the porcelain water-container, pouring a splash of water on the flat piece of slate that apparently served as an ink slab. He selected a stick of ink from the lacquer box, and rubbed off a large quantity of thick, jet-black ink, all the while going over in his mind what he should write. Then he took a few sheets of the heavy, home-made rag-paper that was lying close by the account books, chose a writing brush and wrote out in his bold calligraphy an official communication. When he had finished, he copied out the text a number of times. 'Like writing out lines at school!' he muttered with a wan smile. After he had impressed on each sheet the official seal he always carried suspended by a silk cord on his belt, he rolled the papers up and put them into his sleeve.

Leaning back in his chair, he calculated the chances of success. His entire body was stiff from the long ride and his back was aching, but his mind was alert. All of a sudden he realized that now, for the first time since he had left Pei-chow, his mental apathy had dropped away from him. He had been a fool to give himself over to morose brooding. He must take action. That is what the dear dead he had left in Pei-chow, his faithful old adviser Hoong and she of the Medicine Hill, expected from him. He must evolve other plans for saving the people here in the country house. If his main scheme should fail, he could always give himself up to the bandits, reveal his true identity and promise them a ransom several times the two hundred gold pieces they asked the landowner for. It implied that he would have to pass an uncomfortable time as hostage, with the possibility that they would cut off his ears or fingers to speed up negotiations. However, he knew how to handle those scoundrels. Anyway it was the surest way to a complete success. He got up and walked out into the cold yard again.

The refugees were busy gobbling their gruel. He walked about among them till he found the youngster to whom he had entrusted his horse. Seeing that the boy had just finished his bowl, he asked him to show him the stables.

In the exposed enclosure the blast of the north wind struck them full in the face. No one was about there. He took the youngster into a corner under the lee of the wall, and had a long conversation with him. Finally he asked him a question, and, as the youngster nodded eagerly, the judge gave him the rolled up papers. He patted the boy on his back and said: 'I put my trust in you!' Then he walked back to the courtyard.

Mr Min was standing below the stairs of the main building. 'I have been looking for you everywhere!' he told the judge gruffly. 'My brother asks you to come up now, before we take our evening rice.'

Min took him inside and up a broad staircase next to the

entrance of the hall, to a large, dimly-lit landing on the second floor. There were several doors there, presumably of the family quarters. Mr Min knocked softly on the door on the left. It was opened a crack, and the wrinkled face of an old woman appeared. Min whispered a few words to her. After a while the door was opened wide. Min motioned the judge to follow him inside.

The cloying smell of medicinal herbs hung heavily in the overheated room. It came from a steaming jar that stood upon the large bronze brazier on the floor, in the farthest corner. The brazier was heaped with glowing coals. The simply furnished room was brilliantly lit by two tall brass candelabra on the side table. The back wall was taken up entirely by an enormous canopied bedstead of intricately carved ebony, its heavy brocade curtains drawn apart. Mr Min bade the judge sit down in the armchair at the head of the bed; he himself took the low footstool next to it. The old woman stood herself at the foot, her hands folded in the long sleeves of her dark-grey robe.

Judge Dee looked at the old man who was watching him from his raised pillow with lack-lustre, red-rimmed eyes. They seemed abnormally large in the hollow, deeply lined face. Untidy strands of grey hair stuck to his high, moist forehead, a straggling grey moustache hung over the thin, tightly compressed mouth. A tangled white beard lay on the thick silken coverlet.

'This gentleman is Magistrate Dee, elder brother,' Mr Min spoke softly. 'He was on his way south, to the capital, but was caught by the flood. He . . .'

'I saw it, saw it in the almanac!' the old landowner suddenly said in a high-pitched, quavering voice. 'When the Ninth Constellation crosses the Sign of the Tiger, it means dire disaster. The almanac says so, very clearly. It means disaster, and violence. Violent death.' He closed his eyes, breathing heavily. After a while he went on, his eyes still closed: 'What was it again, the last time that the Sign of the Tiger got crossed? Yes, I was twelve then. Had just started to ride on horseback, I had. The water rose and rose, it came up to the steps of our gatehouse. I saw with my own eyes how . . .' He was interrupted by a racking cough that shook his thin shoulders. The old woman quickly stepped up to the bed, and made her husband drink from a large porcelain bowl.

When the cough had subsided, Mr Min resumed:

'Magistrate Dee has to stay here, elder brother. I was thinking that the side room downstairs might . . .'

Suddenly the old man opened his eyes. Fixing the judge with a brooding stare, he mumbled:

'It all fits. Exactly. The Sign of the Tiger. The Flying Tigers have come, the flood has come, I have fallen ill, and Kee-yü is dead. We shan't be able to bury her, even . . .' He made an ineffectual effort to raise himself to a sitting position; claw-like hands came out from under the coverlet. Sinking back against the pillow, he croaked at Mr Min: 'They will hack her dead body to pieces, the devils, You must try to . . .' He choked. His wife hastily laid her arm round his shoulders. The old man's eyes closed again.

'Kee-yü was my brother's daughter,' Mr Min told the judge in a hurried whisper. 'She was only nineteen, a very gifted girl. But she suffered from bad health. Weak heart, you know. All this excitement was too much for her. Last night, just before dinner, she died. A sudden heart attack. My brother was very fond of her. The sad news caused a serious relapse, he . . .' He let the sentence trail off.

The judge nodded absent-mindedly. He had been looking at the high cupboard against the side wall. By its side stood the usual pile of four clothes boxes, one for each season, then a large iron box, its lid secured by a heavy copper padlock.

As he turned his head, he found the sick man staring at him. There was a crafty gleam now in the large eyes. His wife had gone to the brazier in the corner.

'Yes, that's where the gold was!' the old man cackled with a broad grin. 'Forty shining gold bars, magistrate! The value of two hundred gold pieces!'

'Aster stole it, the lewd slut!' a dry, cracked voice spoke up behind the judge. It was the old woman. She was fixing the sick man with a malevolent stare.

'Aster was the young maidservant,' Min said to the judge with an embarrassed air. 'She disappeared last night. Joined the bandits.'

'Wanted to bed with those beasts. With every single one of them,' the old woman rasped. 'Then clear out. With the gold.'

The judge got up and walked over to the strongbox. He examined it curiously.

'The lock hasn't been forced,' he remarked.

'She had the key, of course!' the old woman snapped.

The thin hand of the old man clutched at her sleeve. He gave her an imploring look. He wanted to speak but only incoherent sounds came from his twitching mouth. Suddenly tears came trickling down his hollow cheeks.

'No, she didn't take it! You must believe me!' he said, sobbing. 'How could I, sick as I am . . . Nobody pities me, nobody!' His wife bent over him and wiped his nose and mouth with a handkerchief. The judge averted his eyes and bent again over the strongbox. It was covered with thick iron plates, and there was not a single scratch on the solid padlock. When he turned to the bed, the old man had regained his composure. He said dully to the judge:

'Only I, my wife and my daughter knew where the key was. Nobody else.' Slowly a sly smile curved his thin, bloodless lips. He stretched out his right hand and felt with thin, spidery fingers along the edge of the bedstead. The wood was carved into an intricate motif of flowers.

'Aster was hanging about here all the time, especially when you had fever!' the old woman said venomously. 'You showed it to her without even knowing it, you!'

The old man chuckled. His thin fingers had closed round a flowerbud carved in the wood. There was a click and a small panel in the edge of the bed opened. In the shallow cavity lay a large copper key. Giggling with childish delight, he made the panel open and close several times in succession.

'A strapping, comely wench!' he cackled. 'Best peasant stock.' A little saliva came dripping from the corner of his mouth.

'You ought to have been thinking about your daughter's marriage, instead of about that hussy!' his wife remarked.

'Oh yes, my dear daughter!' the landowner said, suddenly serious again. 'My dear, so very clever daughter!'

'It was I who arranged everything with the Liang family, it was I who selected the trousseau!' the old woman said in a querulous voice. 'While you, behind my back . . .'

'I mustn't take too much of your time,' the judge interrupted her. He motioned Mr Min to rise.

'Wait,' the sick man shouted all of a sudden. He regarded the judge with eyes that now were hard and wary. Then he said in a steady voice: 'You will stay in Kee-yü's room, magistrate.'

He heaved a deep sigh and closed his eyes again.

As Mr Min took the judge to the door, the old woman squatted down by the brazier and begun to stir the coals with a pair of copper tongs, muttering angrily.

'Your brother is very ill,' the judge remarked to Mr Min while they were descending the staircase.

'He is indeed. But we'll all be dead. Soon. Kee-yü was lucky, she died in peace.'

'Just before her marriage, apparently.'

'Yes, she had been engaged to young Liang, the eldest son of the owner of the large estate beyond the fort, for quite some time. They were to be married next month. Fine young fellow. Not too handsome, but of a staunch character. I met him in the city once, with his father. And now we can't even notify them that she's dead.'

'Where did you put her body?'

'In a temporary coffin, in the Buddhist house chapel. Behind the hall.' Arrived at the bottom of the stairs, Min exclaimed: 'Ha, I see that Yen and Liao are waiting for us already. You don't want to go up to your room first, I suppose? No need to, you know. There's a washroom in the outhouse, just outside the door here.'

Upon re-entering the hall Judge Dee saw that Min, Yen and Liao had seated themselves at the large table in the rear. Now it bore four large earthenware bowls of rice, four platters of pickled vegetables, and one of salted fish.

'Please excuse the poor fare!' Mr Min said, as a half-hearted attempt at observing the customary amenities due to a guest. Raising his chopsticks as the sign to begin, he grumbled: 'Stocks are running low. My brother ought to have seen to it that. . . .' He shook his head and buried his face in his rice bowl.

They ate in silence for a while. The judge was hungry, and he found the simple, solid food much to his taste. The bailiff rose and fetched from the wall table a brown stone jar and four small porcelain cups. As he was pouring the warm wine, the steward gave him an astonished look. He said crossly:

'So it was you who got that jar out, Yen! How can you possibly think of wine, the night after Miss Kee-yü died; and in our present situation too!'

'Why should we let those beastly bandits swill our wine?' the bailiff asked indifferently. 'The best vintage too! You don't object, do you, Mr Min?'

'Go ahead, go ahead!' the fat man mumbled with his mouth full.

The steward bent his head. The judge noticed that the man's hands were trembling. He sipped from the wine and found it of superior quality.

The steward suddenly put his chopsticks down. Darting a worried glance at the judge he said timidly:

'As a magistrate you must have dealt often with robbers and bandits and so on, sir. Couldn't we persuade them to accept a money draft? The landowner has excellent relations with two banking houses in the city and . . .'

'I have never yet heard of bandits accepting anything but cash,' the judge said dryly. The wine had warmed him, and his boots had dried. He rose and took off his fur coat. Underneath he wore a long travelling robe of padded brown cotton, fastened by a broad sash of black silk, wound several times round his waist. As he was laying his fur coat on the wall table he said: 'We shouldn't be too pessimistic about all this, you know! I see more than one possibility of extricating ourselves from our predicament.'

He sat down again and pushed his fur cap back from his brow. Then he put his forearms on the table and resumed, looking levelly at his three companions:

'The bandits are, admittedly, in an ugly mood, because they are convinced your story about the stolen money was a trick. And they are pressed for time, because they must be off on their rafts before the flood subsides. They are afraid of the soldiers in the fort, and frightened men are hard to deal with. You need not expect them to show us any mercy. There's no use in parleying with them either, unless we establish ourselves in a good bargaining position first. I suppose that your

97

tenant farmers do a lot of fishing in the river, in summer?'
As the bailiff and the steward nodded, the judge went on:
'Good. I expect that the bandits will attack us early in the
morning. Tonight, choose a couple of sturdy farmhands who
know about fishing, issue a large drag-net to them, and let
them climb on this side of the roof of the gatehouse. No
one should know about this, because the bandits may well
have a spy among the refugees. When the bandits arrive I
shall go outside and talk to them. I know how to handle their
kind. I shall tell their leader that we are well-armed, but that
we shan't put up any resistance if they spare our lives. They
may enter the house, and collect everything they want, including a lot of gold and silver finery. They'll accept the
proposal, of course. For that will enable them to plunder the
house leisurely, and kill us afterwards. However, as soon as
the leader and his bodyguards have passed through the gate,
our men on the roof will drop the net over them, men and
horses, while we close the gates in the face of the rest of the
bandits. The leader and his bodyguards will be heavily armed,
but when they are in the net we shall disable them easily
enough by means of a few blows with threshing flails. Then
we'll have hostages, and we can start upon serious negotiations.'

'That isn't such a bad idea,' Mr Min said, nodding
slowly.

The steward's face had lit up. But the bailiff pursed his lips
and said worriedly:

'Far too risky! If there should be a hitch, the scoundrels
won't put us to death quickly. They'll torture us!'

Disregarding the frightened exclamations of Min and
Liao, the judge said firmly:

'If anything goes wrong, you just close the gate behind
me. I can look after myself.' He added with a wry smile: 'I
was born under the Sign of the Tiger, you know!'

Mr Min bestowed a thoughtful look on him. After a while he said:

'All right. I'll see to it that the trap is laid. You'll help me, Liao.' He rose briskly and asked: 'Will you see the magistrate up to his room, Yen? I shall go to the watchtower, presently, to take my turn.' To the judge he added: 'We take turns of three hours, you see, watching for an unexpected move of those scoundrels. All the night through.'

'I'll join you, of course,' the judge said. 'Shall I take the watch after you, Mr Min?'

Mr Min protested that they could never accept that, but Judge Dee insisted, and finally it was agreed that the judge should go to the watchtower from midnight to three o'clock. Yen would then take over from him till dawn.

Mr Min and the steward left for the store-room where the fishing nets were kept. The judge laid his fur coat over his shoulder, took up his sword and followed Yen to the stairs. The bailiff took him up to the landing, then they climbed a narrow, creaking staircase in the corner that led up to the third floor. There the judge saw only a passageway ending in a door of solid wooden boards.

Yen halted and said contritely:

'I do regret that the master assigned this room to you, sir. I hope you don't mind sleeping in a room where only last night . . . I could easily find you a room downstairs, the others need not know that . . .'

'This room will do,' the judge cut him short.

The bailiff opened the door and led him inside a dark, ice-cold room. While lighting the candle on the side table, he resumed:

'Well, it's the best furnished room in the house, of course. Miss Kee-yü was a girl of elegant taste, sir. As you can see for yourself.'

He indicated the furnishings of the spacious room with a

99

sweeping gesture. Pointing at the broad sliding doors that
took up most of the wall opposite, he added: 'Outside is a
balcony that runs along the entire breadth of this top floor.
Miss Kee-yü used to sit there on summer nights, enjoying
the moon over the mountains.'

'Was she all alone up here?'

'Yes, there are no other rooms on this floor. Originally it
was a store-room, I heard. But Miss Kee-yü liked the view
and the quiet up here, and the master gave it to her. Although properly she should have stayed in the women's
quarters, of course, in the east wing of the compound. Well,
I'll send Mr Min's old servant up with a tea-basket. Have a
good rest, sir! I shall come and fetch you at midnight.'

When the bailiff had closed the door behind him, Judge
Dee put on his fur coat again, for it was bitterly cold in the
room, and a nasty draught was coming through the sliding
doors. He laid his sword on the rosewood table in the centre
of the thick-piled blue carpet, then leisurely surveyed the
room. In the corner to the right of the entrance stood a
narrow couch, a thin gauze curtain suspended on its four
rosewood posts. Next to it was the customary pile of four
clothes boxes of red lacquered leather, and close by the sliding doors a dressing-table, with a row of small powder boxes
arranged under the round mirror of polished silver. To the
left of the entrance stood a high, oblong music table, with
a seven-stringed lute lying ready on it, then an elegant bookrack of polished spotted bamboo. In the corner by the sliding doors stood a writing-desk of carved ebony. The judge
walked up to it for a closer look at the painting on the wall
there. It represented a branch of plum blossoms, a fine
specimen of the work of a well-known former artist. He
noticed that the ink slab, the brush holder, the paperweight
and all the other writing implements on the desk were

valuable antiques, evidently selected with loving care. The room bore the stamp of a well-defined personality: an educated, refined girl of fastidious taste.

He sat down on the bamboo chair at the centre table, but got up again just in time as the fragile seat began to collapse. The dead girl must have been of slight build. He pulled the heavy ebony seat belonging to the music table up, and sat on that. Stretching his stiff legs, he listened for a while to the howling of the wind round the roof.

Slowly smoothing down his long beard, the judge tried to bring some order to the confused thoughts his brain was teeming with. He was not at all sure that the stratagem of catching the bandit leader by means of the fishing nets would succeed. He had made the proposal mainly in order to encourage old Mr Min, and to rouse him from his fatalistic lethargy. Nor was he sure that the other scheme he had set into motion would be successful. The surest method was still for him to parley with the bandits personally. The government was averse to granting a pardon to bandits in order to obtain the release of a captured official. And quite correctly too, for the procedure damaged their prestige, and encouraged other miscreants to try the same expedient. Yet they would perhaps make an exception in his case, because of his present high rank. And if he came through the experiment alive, he would see to it that the scoundrels got their deserts, in the end. Emboldened by their success, they would certainly again commit acts of violence, and then he would pounce on them. For a pardon covered only past crimes.

He idly wondered who could have stolen the landowner's gold. The embarrassing scene he had witnessed in the sick man's bedroom had shown that the maid had apparently had opportunities for learning the secret of the key's hiding place. But he had perceived undercurrents, the real meaning of which was beyond him. The old man was said to have been very fond of his daughter. Yet he had referred to her once with an evident sneer. And why had he insisted that he, the judge, should stay in the dead girl's room?

He was startled from his musings by a knock on the door. A bent old man clad in a long blue gown of cheap cotton came in. He silently put a padded tea-basket at Judge Dee's elbow, then placed a wooden water bucket by the dressing-table. When he made for the door again the judge motioned him to wait. He asked:

'Was Miss Kee-yü all alone here when she was seized by a heart attack?'

'Yes, sir.' The greybeard started on a long story in some broad dialect that the judge could not follow.

'Speak slowly, man!' he interrupted him peevishly.

'I said that she was lying on the bed there, didn't I?' the old servant asked surlily. 'All dressed up for dinner, she was, in a white gown of thick silk, the best quality. Must have cost a pretty penny, I thought. But she didn't come down for dinner. Mr Yen went up and knocked. She doesn't answer. So Mr Yen goes down again and calls the master and the master calls me. The master and me come up here, and there she's lying on that bed there, as I told you. She's asleep, we think. But no, when the master calls her she says nothing. The master bends over her, he feels her pulse, he lifts her eyelids. "It's her heart that got her," he says, very pale. "Call your wife!" I fetch my old woman and a bamboo stretcher and we carry her down, to the chapel. Quite some weight it was, I tell you! The master calls Mr Liao the steward to help us getting her into a coffin. But the fool is all to pieces over the news, and no use whatsoever. So I say don't bother, we'll manage. And that is what we did.'

'I see,' the judge said. 'Sad affair.'

'Not nearly as sad as coming down here all the way from the city, sir, just to be chopped up by a gang of robbers.

102

Well, I have had a long life and never a day in want, and my sons and daughters have grown up and married, so what should an old body complain of? I always say . . .'

His voice was drowned in the rattling of a torrential rain that suddenly came down on the rooftiles.

'As if we were needing more water still!' the greybeard grumbled and went out.

The judge reflected that, if this downpour continued, it would make the water rise still higher. On the other hand, it would prevent the Flying Tigers from launching a night-attack. With a sigh he went to the dressing-table, and washed his face and hands. Then he pulled out the upper drawer, and rummaged among the various toilet articles for a comb to do his beard and whiskers. He was astonished to see there a small brocade roll. It seemed a strange place to store away a manuscript or a painting. He untied the fastening band and unrolled the scroll. It was an excellent miniature portrait of a young girl. He was just going to roll it up again when his eye fell on the inscription by its side. It read: 'For my daughter Kee-yü, on the occasion of her reaching the age of two times eight.' So this was the dead girl whose room he was occupying now! As she had looked three years ago, at least. He took the painting over to the table, and studied it intently.

The portrait was done from the waist upward, the face turned three-quarters to the observer. She was dressed in a lilac robe with a pattern of plum-blossoms, and in her slender right hand she was carrying a twig of those flowers. The glossy black hair was combed back straight from her forehead, and gathered in a coil in the neck. Her narrow sloping shoulders suggested a thin figure, and there was the suspicion of a slightly bent back. She had a striking face, not beautiful by commonly accepted standards, but strangely fascinating. The brow was a trifle too high, the nose well-shaped but too pronouncedly aquiline, while the pallor of the hollow cheeks and the bloodless thin lips pointed to protracted ill health. It was the intense, compelling stare of the large, intelligent eyes that gave her that strange charm. Strange because there was a possessive, almost hungry gleam in her look that was vaguely disturbing.

The painter must have been no mean artist. He had indeed given the portrait so much life that the judge suddenly felt embarrassed, as if he were in the bedroom of a girl still alive, and who might enter her room at any moment.

Annoyed with himself, the judge put the portrait down. He listened for a while to the clattering rain, trying to discover for himself why exactly the girl's eyes had disturbed him. His eye fell on the bookrack. He quickly got up and went to it. He laid aside at once the standard works one usually finds in a young daughter's room, such as *The Perfect Housewife*, or *Pattern of Lady-like Behaviour*. The collected works of four romantic poets interested him more, for the dog-eared leaves proved that she had eagerly read those poems. Just as he was about to put the volumes back, he checked himself and had a second look at the names of the poets. Yes, all four of them had committed suicide. Pensively tugging at his moustache, he tried to digest the possible meaning of this discovery. Then he inspected the rest of the books. An expression of perplexity came over his face. They were all Taoist works, dealing with the dietary and other disciplines for curing illness and prolonging life, and with alchemist experiments for preparing the Elixir of Longevity. He went back to the table and again studied the portrait, holding it close by the candle.

Now he understood. Suffering from a chronic heart disease, the poor girl had been obsessed by the fear of dying young. Of dying before she had really lived. That morbid fear had made her try to find solace in the works of those four disillusioned, world-weary poets. Hers were hungry eyes, hungry for life. A hunger so strong that it pulled the observer towards her, as it were, in a desperate desire to partake of his life force. He now understood also why she kept the portrait in the drawer of her dressing-table: in order to compare it daily with her reflection in the mirror, searching for new signs of her deteriorating health. A pathetic girl.

Her predilection for the plum-blossom motif was only natural. The small white flowers, blossoming forth from an old and gnarled, seemingly dead branch, were the traditional symbol of spring, when the life force that had lain dormant during the winter came forth again in full bloom. He walked over to the pile of clothes boxes, and opened the upper one. Nearly all the neatly folded robes and dresses had an inwoven or embroidered plum-blossom pattern.

He poured himself a cup of tea and drank it eagerly. Then he took off his cap and placed it on the table, by his sword. He stepped out of his boots and stretched himself out on the bed, still dressed in his fur coat and all his other clothes. Listening to the monotonous sound of the rain, he tried to sleep, but the portrait of the dead girl was constantly before his mind's eye.

'I admit these blossoms are just a bit common, but why shouldn't a person like them, pray?'

Startled, he opened his eyes and raised himself to a sitting position. In the flickering light of the candle he saw that he was all alone in the room. The coy voice had sounded in his dream. It was exactly the question the girl seemed to be asking the observer of her portrait. He resolutely closed his eyes again and abandoned himself to the soothing sound of the rain. Soon his fatigue asserted itself and he fell into a dreamless sleep.

He was awakened by Yen shaking his shoulder. As he

stepped down from the bed he noticed that the sound of the rain had ceased.

'When did it stop raining?' he asked the bailiff while he was adjusting his cap.

'About half an hour ago, sir. There's only a drizzle now. Just before I left the watchtower, I saw light in the caves of the bandits. Don't know what they are at.'

He took the judge down to the hall on the ground floor, lighting the way by a small storm lantern, covered with oil paper. The large open fire had died down to glowing embers, but it was still agreeably warm in the hall.

The pitch-dark, wet courtyard was by contrast even more cold and desolate. Passing close by the gatehouse, the bailiff held up his lantern, and let its light fall on three men, huddled against the wall. 'They have put a dragnet ready on the roof, sir,' he said in a whisper. 'Those three fellows are experienced fishermen, and they can be up on the roof in a trice.'

The judge nodded. He noticed that the wind was dying down.

Keeping close behind Yen, he climbed the narrow, slippery flight of stone steps that led up to the top of the outer wall. Then he followed the bailiff along the battlements to the watch turret built on the south-east corner. A creaking step-ladder led up to the top, where he saw a small platform surrounded by a solid balustrade of heavy logs. The low-hanging eaves of the pointed roof offered additional protection against wind and rain, and against the arrows of an eventual enemy.

'If you sit on this bench here, sir, you are well protected, and you can yet keep an eye on the surrounding country.' Yen put the lantern down on the floor-boards, but he made no move to take his leave.

'You had better have a few hours' rest before taking over the watch from me,' the judge said.

'I don't feel tired at all, sir. It's the excitement, I suppose. Mind if I keep you company a bit?'

'Not at all.' The judge pointed at the bench, and Yen sat down by his side.

'Now you can see them quite clearly, sir! Look, they have lighted a big fire, in front of the largest cave. What would they be doing?'

Judge Dee peered at the mountain slope.

'Heaven knows,' he said with a shrug. 'Probably want to warm themselves.' He looked round in a southerly direction. No light was glimmering in the darkness there, and the only sound heard was the low rumble of the river. He pulled the fur coat closer. Although the wind had abated, it was still very cold up there. Shivering, he said:

'When I was visiting the old landlord I noticed that his mind was wandering now and then. But apart from that he seems to me a shrewd old gentleman.'

'As shrewd as they make them! He is a stern man, but just and considerate, always mindful of the needs of his tenants. No wonder that he is very popular hereabouts. Until he fell ill, I had an easy job here, you know. Mainly making the rounds of the farms now and then to collect the rent and to look into complaints. Life was rather dull—till the flood came, that is! Heavens, wasn't it different, in the city! Do you know our provincial capital, sir?'

'Only passed through there, once or twice. A lively city.'

'Lively is the word! But expensive, too! You need money to go places there, lots of it. And mine is the less favoured branch of the family, you see. My father owns a small tea-shop, it brings in enough for our daily needs, but that's all. The money is here, has been here for many generations. The old man has a vast amount of gold salted away in the city. Not to speak of his investments up-country.'

'Who inherits all that if the old gentleman should die?'

'Now that Miss Kee-yü is dead, it all goes to his younger brother, Mr Min. And the fellow has already more than he can use! But he doesn't mind getting more. Not he!'

After a brief pause the judge asked casually:

'Were you present when they found her dead body?'

'Eh? Present? No, I wasn't. But it was I who discovered that something was wrong. Miss Kee-yü had been rather depressed in the afternoon, it seems, just like all of us, and the old lady said that she went upstairs earlier than usual. When she did not appear in the old lady's quarters for the evening rice, and didn't answer when I went up and knocked on her door, I went down to warn Mr Min. The old fellow went up with his servant, and they found her lying on her bed, fully dressed. Dead.'

'Was there no possibility of her having committed suicide?'

'Suicide? Heavens no! Old Mr Min knows a lot about medicine, he saw at once that she had died from a heart attack. While she was taking a nap, before dinner. I informed the old master and his wife. Not a pleasant task, I assure you! The old man had another bad attack, and his wife had the devil of a time to calm him down again. Well, in the meantime Mr Min had the body placed in the spare coffin, in the house chapel. And that was that.'

'I see,' Judge Dee said. 'When I paid my visit to the land-owner, his wife said something about a maid called Aster. She suggested that Aster had known the secret hiding place of the gold, and that she had absconded with it. I didn't quite understand what it was all about.'

'Well, it does seem the most likely explanation of the disappearance of the gold, sir. It was kept in a strongbox in the master's bedroom, forty shining gold bars, equalling two hundred gold pieces. The key was hidden in a secret panel, in the master's bedstead. Only he and his wife knew the place.

Now, Aster is an uneducated girl, but a pretty piece of goods, and as shrewd as some of those peasant girls are. She made up to the old man, let him fondle her a bit now and then, I suppose, hoping to be installed as a concubine, sooner or later.'

Yen made a face, and resumed: 'Anyway, he showed her where he kept the key, or talked about it when he was delirious with fever. When the bandits arrived, Aster thought that one bird in the hand is better than two in the bush, took the gold and ran off. She buried the gold bars under a tree or under a rock, then went to the bandits. Those dogs would welcome a nice strapping wench, of course. Later on she could run off, collect the gold, and marry a wealthy shopkeeper in the next province. Not a bad deal, if you come to think of it! Well, I had better turn in, after all. Do you see that bronze gong hanging from the rafters? Should the bastards come down here, you beat it with the club hanging next to it. That is our alarm signal. I'll be back on time! No, thank you, I don't need the lantern, I know my way about.'

Judge Dee turned the bench round and sat down, his folded arms on the balustrade, facing the dark mountain slope. He knew exactly what the Flying Tigers were at, for he had seen the stakes the tiny black figures in front of the fire were moving about. He had not told Yen Yuan, in order not to frighten him—although the fellow seemed the least disturbed of all the inmates of the country house. The bandits were in fact constructing a battering-ram. But he did not think they would attack before dawn unless the sky cleared and the moon came out, of course. He could do nothing but wait.

What the bailiff had just told him about the death of Kee-yü tallied with what Mr Min's old servant had said. Yet he had the uncomfortable feeling that there had been more there than met the eye. The old landowner must have suspected something of that kind; that was the only explanation of the sick man's eagerness to let him, a magistrate, stay in his dead daughter's room. The old man evidently hoped that he, as an experienced criminal investigator, would discover there clues that would throw a new light on her demise.

It was curious that the landowner had quoted the almanac on stellar portents. The almanac was drawn up every year by the Board of Rites, and all passages on the occult meaning of the signs appearing in the sky during the coming year were drawn up after a careful study of the Book of Divination. These indications were therefore not to be lightly dismissed, for they embodied the wisdom of the Ancients. He himself had been born under the Sign of the Tiger. Was it the mystic influence of this animal of the zodiac that had brought him here to this lonely house tonight?

Shaking his head he decided that it was better to leave occult considerations alone, and to concentrate on factors subject to human control. What the old man had said about portents pointing to violent death, could have referred to the impending attack of the Flying Tigers as well as to his daughter's sudden demise. It was a great pity that no competent doctor had been present. Mr Min had doubtless a fair knowledge of medicine, most elderly householders had, it used to be part of their general education. But he could not be compared to a professional physician, of course, and certainly not to a coroner. The judge himself was thoroughly familiar with forensic medicine and he would have liked to do an autopsy on the dead girl. But that was of course out of the question.

Then he thought about his retinue, left at the gap. He hoped it would have proved possible to maintain the bridge-head, so that the soldiers could pass the night in the barracks there. He was a bit worried about the two Senior Investigators from the capital who had brought to Pei-chow the

Imperial Decree concerning his promotion and who were now part of his retinue. Born and bred in the capital, they were accustomed to travel in comfort. This made him think of his wives and children. It was fortunate that they had still been in his native place when the news of his promotion arrived in Pei-chow. The day he left there he had ordered his assistant Tao Gan to stay behind to receive his successor, and sent his trusted lieutenants Ma Joong and Chiao Tai to Tai-yuan, to inform his First Lady and escort her, his two other wives and his children direct to the capital. It was a safe route, he need not worry about them.

Time passed surprisingly fast. Sooner than he had expected the bailiff's head appeared again at the head of the stepladder.

'Anything new?' Yen asked eagerly as he stepped on to the platform.

'Nothing,' the judge replied. 'But it looks as if the sky is going to clear. If that should happen, you had better keep a close watch on those scoundrels over there.'

He picked up the lantern and went down.

When he was about to enter the main building, he met the steward Liao. The gaunt man was coming from the stable yard.

'I thought I heard the horses neigh, and went to see whether the stables were dry. When will the bandits come, do you think, sir? This terrible waiting . . .'

'Hardly before dawn. Isn't it very cold in those outhouses over there? What about the women and children among the refugees?'

'They are all right, sir. The walls are heavy, and we put a thick layer of straw on the floor.'

The judge nodded and went inside. The fire in the hall had gone out now; it was stone cold there. All was quiet as the grave. Aided by his lantern, he found his way up to the landing on the second floor without difficulty. Then he climbed the stairs to the third floor, treading carefully in order to avoid the creaking steps.

Upon entering the dead girl's room he was surprised to find it lit by a silvery, diffuse light. It came from the paper panes of the sliding doors. He crossed the room and pushed the doors open. The moon had come out, bathing the mountain scene in its white, eerie light.

He stepped out on the balcony. The floorboards and the plain wooden balustrade were still wet with the rain. At the extreme left was a bamboo flower rack. A few empty pots stood on the three shelves, one above the other, like library steps.

Now he could see clearly that it was indeed a battering-ram the bandits were working on. He did not think, however, that they could have it ready before dawn, for they had to construct a wheelcart too, in order to bring the ram down the slope and up to the gatehouse. Leaning over the balustrade, he saw, about twenty feet below, the roofs of the buildings in the back part of the compound. He looked up. The broad eaves of the roof hung over the balcony. Above the lintel of the sliding doors there was a row of wooden panels about three feet square, each carved with an intricate design of dragons sporting among clouds. He reflected that this careful finishing of all details proved that the country house was at least two hundred years old. Later architects did not spend so much loving care on such details any more.

There was a pleasant nip in the air; it looked as if the frost might set in again before long. He decided to leave the doors half open. That would also help him to hear the gong better, should there be an alarm. He was about to prepare himself for bed, but changed his mind when his eye fell on the music table at the back of the room. He did not feel sleepy, really, and trying his hand at the lute would help him to pass the

HE PULLED THE SILK STRINGS IN SUCCESSION

time. Besides, all the old lute handbooks recommended a moonlit night as the most suitable time for playing this instrument. He had played the seven-stringed lute in his youth, for it had been the favourite musical instrument of the Immortal Sage Confucius, and its study was part of the literary education. But the judge had not touched the strings for many years. He was curious to see whether he could still remember the complicated finger technique.

He pulled the music table round and placed the ebony seat behind it so that he sat with his back to the wall. Massaging and flexing his cold fingers, he examined the instrument with interest. The red laquer of the flat, oblong soundbox was covered with small bursts, indicating that this particular instrument was at least a hundred years old, and a valuable antique. He pulled with his forefinger the seven silk strings in succession. The lute had an uncommonly deep tone, its vibrating notes echoed in the silent room. The tuning was still approximately correct, which proved that she must have played it shortly before her death. While he adjusted it by turning the agate pegs on his right hand, he tried to remember the opening of one of his favourite melodies. But when he had started to play he soon realized that, although he remembered the melody quite clearly, he had forgotten the finger technique. He pulled out the drawer where lute players usually keep their musical scores. Leafing through the slender volumes, he found only the more difficult classical compositions, which would be far beyond him. There were several copies of the well-known melody 'Three Variations on the Plum-blossom Motif'—which was only to be expected since the dead girl had been so fond of those flowers. At the bottom of the drawer he discovered the score of a brief, rather simple melody, which bore the title of 'Autumn in the Heart'. He had never seen it before and the words, written by the side of the notation in a small, neat

114

hand, were completely new to him. A few words had been crossed out, and the score had been corrected here and there. Evidently this was one of the dead girl's own compositions. The song consisted of two parts:

The yellowing leaves
Come drifting down
Weaving a gown
For the last autumn rose.
Silent autumn
Weighs down the heart
The hungry heart
That finds no repose.

The yellowing leaves
Drift in the breeze
Frightening away
The last autumn geese.
Would they could take me
On their long flight home
To the distant home
Where the heart finds peace.

He played the melody through once, very slowly, his eyes glued to the score. There was a lilt in it that made it easy to memorize. After he had repeated the more difficult bars a few times, he knew the tune by heart. He shook the cuffs of his fur coat back from his wrists and prepared to play it seriously, raising his head to the moonlit mountain scene outside.

All of a sudden he stopped playing. Out of the corner of his eye he had seen a slender girl, standing by the desk in the left corner. The grey shape was shrouded in shadows, but the bent shoulders and the profile with the curved nose, and the hair combed back straight from the brow were clearly outlined against the moonlit screen door.

For the barest instant the grey shape hovered there. Then it dissolved into the shadows.

Judge Dee sat motionless, his hands resting on the silken strings. He wanted to call out, but a tight feeling was constricting his throat. Then he got up, stepped round the lute table and slowly advanced a few paces in the direction of the left corner where the shape had disappeared. Dazedly he stared at the desk. No one was there.

He rubbed his hand over his face. It must have been the ghost of the dead girl.

With an effort he pulled himself together. He pushed the sliding doors wide open, and stepped out on the narrow balcony. There he took a deep breath of the cold crisp air. In his long career he had on occasion met with ghostly phenomena, but those had proved to have a perfectly natural explanation, in the end. However, how could there be a rational explanation of the dead girl's apparition he had witnessed just now? Could it have been a figment of his imagination, just as when he thought he had heard the dead girl address him, after he had lain himself down to sleep? But then he had been dozing, whereas now he was wide awake.

Slowly shaking his head, he went inside again, pulling the sliding doors closed behind him. He took his tinderbox from his sleeve and lit the small storm lantern. He had made up his mind. The ghostly apparition could mean only one thing : that the girl had died a violent death here in this room. Her disembodied spirit was still roaming about, and trying desperately to manifest itself, overcoming the barrier that separates the dead from the living. While he was falling asleep she had succeeded in getting her voice across to him. Just now, when he was concentrating his mind on the melody she had composed herself, the contact had suddenly been established, enabling her to project her shape for one brief moment in the world of the living. His duty was clear. He took the lantern and went downstairs.

On the landing on the first floor he halted. A strip of light came from under the door of the sick man's room. He tiptoed up to it and pressed his ear to the panel. There was a low murmur of voices, but he could distinguish no words. After a while the murmur ceased. Then someone began to intone a low chant, resembling a magic incantation, or a prayer.

He descended into the hall. Standing at the bottom of the staircase, he lifted his lantern to orientate himself. Apart from the main entrance, he remembered having seen only one other door down there, behind his chair when he was having dinner. That seemed to tally with Mr Min's remark that the house chapel was at the back of the hall.

He walked across the hall and rattled at the door. It was not locked. As he opened it, the heavy smell of Indian incense told him that his assumption had been correct. He closed the door noiselessly behind him, and held the lantern high. Against the back wall of the small room stood a high altar table of red-lacquered wood, on it a small shrine containing a gilded statue of Kwan Yin, the Goddess of Mercy. In front of her he saw a silver incense burner. Four incense sticks were standing in the ash it was half filled with, their ends glowing.

The judge fixedly regarded the sticks. Then he pulled one from the bundle of new sticks lying by the burner, and compared its length with that of those burning in the vessel. The latter proved to be only a quarter of an inch shorter. That meant that the person who had lighted the sticks must have visited the chapel only a short while ago.

He pensively looked at the oblong box of unpainted wood which was standing on two trestles; this was the spare coffin

117

the dead girl's body had been placed in. The wall opposite was covered from floor to ceiling by a fine antique brocade hanging, embroidered with the scene of Buddha's entry into Nirvana. The dying Buddha was reclining on a couch; representatives of all beings of the three worlds surrounded him, bemoaning his departure.

The judge put his lantern on the altar table. He reflected that, since the door of the chapel had not been locked, anyone who liked could have gone in. Suddenly he had the uncomfortable feeling that he was not alone. Yet no one could have hidden himself in that small room. Unless there was an empty space behind the wall hanging. He stepped up to it, and pressed it with his forefinger. It was hanging directly against the solid wall. He shrugged. There was no use in speculating who could have visited the chapel before him. But he had better be quick, for the unknown visitor might come back.

He walked round the prayer cushion in the centre of the floor, and by the light of the lantern looked the coffin over. It was about six feet long but only two feet high, so he would probably be able to examine the dead body without having to remove it from the coffin. He noticed with satisfaction that the lid had not been nailed down, it was fastened only by a broad strip of oiled paper that had been pasted down all around it. But the lid looked fairly heavy, it would not be easy to remove it, all by himself.

He took off his fur coat, folded it and laid it on the floor. He didn't need it, for the air was close, and it was fairly warm in the small room. Then he bent over the coffin. Just as he was testing the edge of the paper band with his long thumbnail, he heard a sigh.

Frozen in his attitude, he strained his ears, but heard only the pounding of his own blood. It must have been the rustling of the wall hanging, for he noticed there was a slight

118

SUDDENLY THE JUDGE HAD THE FEELING THAT HE WAS
NOT ALONE

draught. He began to loosen the paper band. Then suddenly a black shadow fell on the lid.

'Leave her in peace!' a hoarse voice spoke up behind him. The judge swung round. The steward stood there, staring at him with wide eyes.

'I must examine Miss Kee-yü's dead body,' the judge said gruffly. 'I suspect foul play. You wouldn't know about that, would you? Why did you come here?'

'I . . . I couldn't sleep. I had gone to the yard because I thought . . .'

'That the horses were neighing. You told me that already when I met you out there. Answer my question!'

'I came to burn incense here, sir. For the rest of Miss Kee-yü's soul.'

'Commendable loyalty to your master's daughter. If that were true, why did you hide when I came in? And where?'

The steward pulled the wall hanging aside. With a trembling hand he pointed at the niche in the wall, close by the farthest corner.

'There . . . there was a door there, formerly,' he stammered. 'It was walled up.' Turning to the coffin, he went on slowly: 'Yes, you are right. I did not need to hide. There is no need to hide anything any more. I was deeply in love with her, sir.'

'And she with you?'

'I never let her know my feeling of course, sir!' the steward exclaimed, aghast. 'It is true that my family was well known, half a century ago. But it declined, and I haven't got a penny of my own. How could I ever dare to tell the landowner that I . . . Besides, she was engaged to be married, to the son of . . .'

'All right. Now, tell me, do you think there was something wrong about her sudden death?'

'No sir. Why should there be anything wrong? We all knew that she had a weak heart, and the excitement of . . .'

'Quite. Did you see her dead body?'

'I couldn't have born that sight, sir! Never! I wanted to remember her as she was, always so . . . so . . . Mr Min asked me to help him and the old servant to place her in this . . . this coffin, but I couldn't, I was so upset. First the bandits, and then this, this sudden . . .'

'Well, you'll help me now to remove the lid, anyway!'

The judge loosened the end of the strip, then tore it down with a few jerks.

'You lift the other end!' he ordered. 'Then we'll let it down on the floor.'

Together they raised the lid.

All of a sudden the steward let his end go. The lid dropped back, half across the coffin. The judge just managed to prevent it from falling onto the floor.

'It isn't Kee-yü!' the steward shrieked. 'It's Aster!'

'Shut up!' the judge barked. He stared at the still face of the girl in the coffin. It was not without a certain vulgar beauty, even in death. Rather heavy eyebrows curved above the bluish lids of the closed eyes, the round cheeks had dimples, the full mouth was well-shaped. It did not in the least resemble Kee-yü's portrait.

'Let's put the lid down on the floor without too much noise,' he told the shivering steward quietly.

After he had let the heavy lid down onto the floor, the judge took the lantern and set it on a corner of the coffin. He pensively regarded the long white robe. It was of good silk, with a woven plum-blossom pattern. The sash had been tied directly below the generous bosom, in the customary elaborate, triple bow. The arms lay stiffly by the body's sides.

'The robe belongs to Miss Kee-yü all right,' the judge remarked.

'It does indeed, sir. But it's Aster, I tell you! What happened to Miss Kee-yü?'

'We'll get to that presently. First I must examine this corpse. You wait outside, in the hall. Don't light the candle, I don't want anyone to know about this yet.'

The frightened steward began to protest with chattering teeth, but the judge pushed him unceremoniously outside, and closed the door.

He set to work on the bow of the sash. It took him some time before he had loosened the complicated knots. Then he put his left arm under the waist and raised the body a little so that he could remove the sash that had been wound several times round her torso. The body was quite heavy. This tallied with the old servant's complaint about the weight of the body he and Mr Min carried downstairs. He hung the sash over the edge of the box and pulled the robe open in front. She had no underwear, so that the shapely naked body was now entirely exposed. He took the lantern and examined it inch by inch, looking for signs of violence. But the smooth, white skin was whole, there were only a few superficial scratches on the large breasts, and here and there on the rounded belly. After he had established that she had been in about the fourth month of pregnancy, he pulled the stiff arms out of the wide sleeves. He cast a brief glance at the short, broken nails and the calluses on the hand palms, then turned the body on its side. He suppressed a cry. Just below the left shoulderblade there was a small black plaster, about the size of a copper coin. He carefully peeled it off. The discoloured flesh underneath showed a small wound. The judge studied it for a long time, feeling the flesh around it and finally probing the depth with a toothpick. She had been murdered. And with a long, thin knife, the point of which must have penetrated into the heart.

After he had laid the body on its back again he pulled the robe up over it. He tried to re-tie the triple sash-bow, but could not manage it. So he just tied the ends together in a simple knot. He looked down on the white shape for a while, his arms folded in his long sleeves, his bushy eyebrows knitted in a deep frown. It was all very puzzling indeed.

He opened the door and called the steward. Liao was trembling violently and his face had a deadly pallor. Together they replaced the lid on the coffin.

'Where is your room?' the judge asked while putting his fur coat on again.

'At the back of the compound, sir. Next to that of Mr Yen Yuan.'

'Good. Go straight to bed. I'll make a search for Miss Kee-yü.'

Forestalling any questions the judge turned round and left the chapel. At the entrance of the hall he dismissed the steward with a few kind words, then mounted the broad staircase.

Light came from the landing above. Mr Min was standing in front of the sick man's room, a tall candlestick in his hand. His broad, heavy-jowled face was as haughty as ever, and he was still clad in his long grey robe. He bestowed a baleful look on the judge and asked gruffly:

'Had your spell up in the watchtower?'

'I did. Nothing new. How is your brother, Mr Min?'

'Hm. I was just going to have a look. But since there's no light, I'd better go back to my own room. Wouldn't do to wake up his wife, she'll be dozing in the armchair by the bed. Woman is dog-tired. You had better have a good sleep too. No earthly use in gadding about. Good night.'

The judge looked after the portly gentleman as he shuffled

to the door at the end of the landing. Then he climbed the stairs to the third floor.

Back in Kee-yü's room, he put the lantern on the table and remained standing there for a while, staring at the moonlit panes of the sliding doors. If Kee-yü was alive, he could well have seen a fleeting glimpse of her shadow, cast on the outside of the door screen, and have mistaken it for a ghostly shape *inside* the room. If that were true, she must have been watching him from the balcony.

He pulled the sliding doors open and stepped outside. His previous examination of the situation out there had proved that it would be impossible to climb up on the balcony from below, or to let oneself down there from the roof. And since he had gone out on to the balcony very soon after seeing the apparition, there had been no time for using ladders. He turned round and looked up at the row of carved panels running above the lintel of the sliding doors. He quickly went inside again, and found that the ceiling of the room was only an inch or two above the lintel. That meant that between ceiling and roof there was a loft, only three feet high under the eaves, but increasing in height as the roof sloped upward to the top. Walking out on the balcony again, he gave the flower rack at the left end a thoughtful look. Suppose that there was an entrance to the loft up there? One could easily reach the panels by using the rack as a step-ladder.

He tested the lowest shelf with his foot. It was much too fragile to support his weight, but it would probably support a slight young girl all right. He fetched the ebony seat of the lute table from inside, and placed it close by the flower rack. The carved panels were now within easy reach. He felt the edge of the one just above the rack, and discovered he could move it aside a bit. When he exercised more pressure, the panel slid open. The light of his lantern fell on the pale, frightened face of the girl crouching just inside the dark opening.

'You had better come down, Miss Min,' the judge said dryly. 'You need not be afraid, I am a guest of your father staying here overnight. Here, let me give you a hand.'

But she did not need any assistance. She put her foot down on the upper shelf of the flower rack and lightly descended. Gathering her dust-covered blue robe around her, she cast a quick glance at the mountain slope where the fires of the bandits were burning high. Then she went silently inside.

The judge motioned her to take the chair by the table, then sat down opposite her, on the lute-seat, which he had dragged inside again. Stroking his long, greying beard, he studied her pale, drawn face. She had not much changed in the last three years. He marvelled again at the skill of the painter who had achieved that perfect likeness. And the pose from the waist upward had been cleverly contrived. It had glossed over the bent back that was nearly a hump, and it concealed the fact that her head was a little too large for the small, frail body. At last he spoke:

'I was told that you had died from a heart attack, Miss Min. Your old parents are mourning for you. In fact, it was the maid Aster who died here in this room. She was murdered.' He paused. When she remained silent, he resumed: 'I am a magistrate, from a district up north. This place does not belong to my territory, of course, but since it is completely isolated now, I represent the law here. Therefore, it is my duty to investigate this murder. Please explain what happened.'

She raised her head. There was a sombre gleam in her wide eyes.

'Does it matter?' she asked in a low, cultured voice. 'We

125

shall all be murdered. Soon. Look, the red glow of dawn is in the sky.'

'The truth always matters, Miss Min. I am waiting for your explanation.'

She shrugged her narrow shoulders. 'Last night, before dinner, I had come up here. I washed and made up my face, waiting for Aster to come and help me change. When she did not appear, I got up and went out on the balcony. Standing on the balustrade, I watched the mountain slope, looking for those awful bandits, and thinking worriedly about what would happen to us. At last, when I had been standing there for a considerable time, I realized that it was getting late, and decided to change my robes without waiting for Aster. When I had gone inside, I saw Aster lying on my bed, on her right side, her back turned to me. With an angry remark on my lips I stepped up to the bed. Then I saw to my horror that the back of her dress was stained with blood. I bent over her. She was dead.

'I began to shriek, but quickly put my hand over my mouth. In a flash I realized what must have happened. When Aster came up and didn't find me in the room, she thought that I was still somewhere downstairs. She laid herself down on my bed, planning to jump up as soon as she would hear me coming. She was that kind of impertinent, lazy girl, you know. Then someone came in and killed her, thinking it was me. Just when that awful thought had come to me, I heard shuffling footsteps on the landing outside. That must be the murderer coming back! In a panic I rushed out on the balcony, and up into the loft.'

She paused and pensively patted her hair with her slender white hand. Then she went on:

'I must explain that I had been exploring the possibilities of that loft, as soon as I learnt that the bandits had come. I wanted to ascertain whether it could serve as a hiding place

126

for my old parents and me, should the bandits come and ransack the house. It seemed eminently suited for that purpose, so I put a few coverlets there, a water jar, and some boxes of dried fruit. Well, I hadn't left my bedroom one moment too soon. For now I heard the door open, and again those horrible, shuffling footsteps. I waited for a long time, straining my ears, but I heard nothing. At last there came a loud knocking on the door, and someone shouted for me. I thought it was a trick of the murderer, who had discovered his mistake, so I kept quiet. Then there were again loud knocks on the door. I heard my uncle cry out in alarm that I was dead. My uncle had mistaken Aster for me. He had not met me after his arrival here, and the last time he had seen me had been seven years ago. Nor had he seen Aster, who had kept to the women's quarters that afternoon. Yet it was strange that my uncle made that mistake, for Aster had been wearing her blue maid's dress. I concluded that the murderer, when he came back the second time, had undressed the dead body and clad it in one of my robes. I wanted to come out and tell my uncle everything, then I reflected that it was much better to leave the murderer under the impression that I had disappeared, thus giving me time to try to obtain a clue to his identity.

'Exhausted by fear and suspense, I slept that whole night. This morning I came down once to fetch a new jug of water and a box of cakes. I crept down to the landing on the second floor, and overheard the bailiff and the steward discussing my sudden death, from a heart attack. That proved to me that the murderer had somehow or other succeeded in obliterating the traces of his cruel deed, and that made me all the more afraid. For he must be an uncommonly resourceful and ruthless man. In the afternoon I slept. In the evening I heard voices in my room, one I recognized as that of the bailiff. Then all was quiet again, until I heard someone playing my lute, my own favourite melody. Since no one in the house plays the lute except me, I suspected it might be someone from outside, either the murderer or an accomplice. The rainstorm was over, so this seemed an excellent opportunity for trying to learn who my unknown enemy was. I climbed down noiselessly and peered round the screen door. In the shadows in the back of the room I saw a tall bearded man completely unknown to me. In a dead fright I fled up to my hiding place again. That is all, sir.'

Judge Dee nodded slowly. She was an intelligent girl, capable of logical reasoning. He pulled the tea-basket towards him and poured her a cup. He waited till she had emptied it eagerly, then asked:

'Who wanted to kill you, do you think, Miss Min?'

She shook her head disconsolately.

'No one I can think of, sir. That's exactly what frightens me so, that terrible uncertainty! I hardly know anybody from outside, for we have few visitors here, you know. Until last year a music master used to come here regularly from the village by the fortress, and my teacher in painting and calligraphy lived in for some time. Then, when my studies had been completed, and after my impending marriage to young Mr Liang had been announced, I led a very secluded life and saw no one that did not belong to the household.'

'In such a case,' the judge remarked, 'we always begin by looking for a motive. Am I right in assuming that you are the sole heir to the estate?'

'Yes, I am. I had an elder brother, but he died, three years ago.'

'Who would be the next heir?'

'My uncle, sir.'

'That might constitute a strong motive. I was told that, although your uncle is a wealthy man, he still is very fond of money.'

'Oh no, not uncle!' she cried out. 'He has always been very close to my father, he would never . . . No, you may dismiss that idea at once, sir.' She thought for a while. After some hesitation, she resumed: 'There's Mr Liao, our steward, of course. I know he was fond of me. He never said so, of course, but I knew it all right. It's true that a man in his subordinate position, and without property, would ordinarily not even dream of marrying his master's only daughter. But since Liao comes from an old literary family that produced two eminent poets, there was a chance that my father, if I had been agreeable, would have considered an eventual proposal. However, Liao kept silent, and when my engagement to Mr Liang had been announced, it was of course too late. That news upset him greatly, I couldn't fail to notice that. But it seems unthinkable that such a modest, refined gentleman as Mr Liao would ever . . .'

She gave the judge a questioning look, but he made no comment. He took a sip from his tea, then said:

'I don't think that Aster was murdered by mistake, Miss Min. I am convinced that it was indeed she who was the murderer's intended victim. I examined her dead body just now, and found that she was pregnant. Have you any idea who could have been the father of her unborn child?'

'Any man she met!' Kee-yü said venomously. 'She was a lazy, lewd girl, always romping with the young farmhands in the backyard. She thought that nobody knew about her disgraceful behaviour, but I saw it with my own eyes, from the balcony up here. Disgusting, it was! Just like a common streetwalker! And it was she who stole the gold. We thought that she had run away with it. But as soon as I knew that she had been murdered, I realized that the gold must still be here, hidden somewhere in the house. Yes, you are right of course, sir! It was not a murder by mistake! It was her paramour who killed her, to get all the gold! We must find it, sir. Our life depends upon it!'

The judge refilled their cups. 'I heard,' he remarked casually, 'that Aster was a simple, steady girl who looked after your sick father quite well.'

Her face went red with anger.

'She? Look after him? I shall tell you what she did, the insolent hussy! Tried to sell her body to him, that's what she did! My mother had to chase her out of father's room, time and again. I myself once caught her there, straightening the quilts she was, she said. But she ought to have straightened her robe! It was hanging wide open in front; she was showing those fat breasts of hers! That's how she came to know about the key of the strongbox, the sly slut! And all the time that she was toadying up to father, she was playing her sordid little games with a vagabond she met in the fields! And he got her with child. You must interrogate those wretched refugees, sir; the fellow must have sneaked inside here with them. He killed her, to get the stolen gold.'

'Well,' the judge said slowly, 'I do believe that she was murdered by the father of her unborn child. But I don't believe it was just a vagabond. A vagabond could never have had the opportunity for killing her up in your room here. It must have been someone who belonged to the household, who could come and go without anyone's questioning him. That man thought that he was alone with Aster up here when he stabbed her to death. But after he had gone downstairs, he noticed that you weren't there, and he then realized that you must have been out on the balcony all the time, and most probably witnessed the crime. He decided to frighten you into silence. That's why he came up here again, and dressed Aster's body in your robe. In order to warn you that he would kill you too if you opened your mouth. He must be a very worried man by now. Who knew about your hiding place in the loft, Miss Min?'

'Absolutely nobody, sir. I had planned to tell my father last night, after dinner.'

'Quite.' The judge got up and went out on the balcony. In the grey light he saw that the wheelcart for the battering-ram was ready now. The Flying Tigers were leading their horses out of the cave. He sat down again and said:

'There aren't so many persons to choose our murderer from, really. I think that Yen Yuan, the bailiff, is our most likely suspect.' Cutting Kee-yü's protests short by quickly raising his hand, he went on: 'His scant interest in the dead body is suspicious. It makes one think he deliberately avoided seeing it, and not because of the sentimental reason that moved the steward Liao. Yen didn't want to run the risk of being asked why he didn't tell Mr Min that the body was not yours—should something go wrong. For, unlike Mr Min and his old servant, the bailiff, of course, knew you and Aster very well.'

She gave the judge a horrified look.

'Mr Yen is a well-educated, serious young man!' she cried. 'How could he ever so debase himself as to have an affair with a common country wench?'

'I am better qualified than you to assess such entangle-ments, Miss Min,' the judge said gently. 'Yen impresses me as a man of loose morals, who reluctantly left the city lights. I suspect that his father sent him here because of some sordid amorous affair that made a prolonged absence from the city desirable. His father thus condoned that one mistake. A second one, namely seducing a maidservant in the house of a relative, might well have resulted in his father's expelling him from the family.'

'Nonsense!' she exclaimed angrily. 'Yen had been ill, and he was sent out here for a change of air.'

'Come now, Miss Min! An intelligent girl like you can't possibly believe such a thin story!'

'It is not a thin story!' she said stubbornly. Rising, she resumed: 'Would you now take me to my father, sir? I am anxious to tell him everything. And I also want to consult with him about making another search for the gold. For that is our only hope left. If we don't find it, and quickly too, the bandits will murder all of us!'

Judge Dee got up also.

'I shall gladly take you to your parents, Miss Min. However, before doing so, I want you to accompany me to the watchtower. I shall question Mr Yen, and I want you to be present so that I can verify his statements at once. If he proves to be innocent, we must try to discover the gold by ourselves.' Seeing that she was about to protest, he pointed outside and exclaimed: 'Heavens, they are coming!'

With the frightened girl close by his side, he stared at the dozen or so horsemen that came galloping down the mountain slope. A wooden structure on wheels came behind them. Other bandits were crowding around it, checking its descent.

'They are bringing their battering-ram down!' the judge said excitedly. He grabbed her sleeve and snapped: 'Hurry up, time is pressing!'

'What about the gold?' she cried out.

'Yen will tell us. Come on!'

He dragged the hesitating girl along. As they were rushing downstairs, the alarm gong in the watchtower began to clang. They quickly crossed the yard, where the refugees came pouring out of their quarters, babbling excitedly. While ascending the steep ladder in the watchtower the judge saw out of the corner of his eye two sturdy youngsters climb on the roof of the gatehouse where a large drag-net was lying ready.

'They are coming down, with a ram!' the bailiff shouted when Judge Dee appeared on the platform. 'They have . . .'

He broke off in mid-sentence, looking with open mouth at Kee-yü, who was coming up behind the judge.

'You . . . you . . .' he stammered.

'Yes, I am alive, as you see,' she said quickly. 'I had found a hiding place in the loft, and the magistrate fetched me from there. You did not see the dead body, so you did not know it wasn't me. It was Aster.'

Confused shouts resounded outside the wall, below. Four horsemen were riding up and down there in the grey morning light. They mockingly waved their spears, their tiger-skin capes fluttering in the breeze. The judge looked round at the broad expanse of the muddy river. The water seemed to have risen still higher after the rainstorm. But the mist had cleared; he thought he saw a black spot, in the distance.

Turning to the bailiff, he said harshly:

'Everything has become crystal-clear now, Mr Yen. You and Kee-yü murdered Aster together. She was with child by you, and pressed you to marry her. But your affair with that poor peasant girl had just been a little amusement on the side. You were counting on marrying Miss Kee-yü, the heiress. Kee-yü loved you passionately, but she knew that her father would never give his consent to your marrying her. Kee-yü had been solemnly betrothed to Mr Liang, and he would never give her to a penniless wastrel who was moreover a relative. The arrival of the Flying Tigers suggested an excellent solution of your problem. Kee-yü stole the gold and hid it in a safe place. Then you two murdered Aster. You dressed her in one of Kee-yü's robes; there was no time for putting on underclothes too. Kee-yü hid herself in the loft. You, Mr Yen, would take the necessary measures to

133

prevent anyone else but Mr Min and his old servant from seeing the dead body, and to have it encoffined as soon as possible. Thus everybody would assume that it was Kee-yü who had died. The small stab-wound in Aster's back had been carefully cleaned, and a plaster pasted over it. If Mr Min should have a look at her back, he would think that the plaster had been put on when she was still alive, and that it covered a scratch or something small like that. In fact he did not undress her; there was no reason to, for why should the thought of murder have entered his mind? Since he did not undress her, he did not see that she was not wearing any underclothes—a fact that might have set him thinking.'

'What a story!' Kee-yü said with disdain. 'Well, what would we have done afterwards, according to your fantastic theory?'

'That's simple. When the Flying Tigers were storming this house, Yen would disappear in the general confusion, and join you up in the loft. After the bandits had put everybody to the sword, ransacked the house and left, you two would come out of your hiding place, and wait till the flood had subsided. You knew that the bandits would not set the house on fire, as is their custom, for they would fear that the blaze would attract the attention of the sentries of the fort. Then you two would flee together to the city, with the gold, of course. Having lain low there for a suitable period, Kee-yü would go to the tribunal, with a long tale of woe: that she had been kidnapped by the Flying Tigers, who led her a terrible life till at last she succeeded in escaping from their clutches. Then she would claim the estate, as the rightful heir. The two of you could go to some distant place, get married and live happily ever after. You would have sacrificed your old parents and about fifty other persons, but I don't think that would have bothered you very much.'

As Kee-yü and the bailiff remained silent, the judge resumed:

'Well, it was your bad fortune that I had to ask for shelter here last night. I discovered the murder, and I located you, Miss Min, in your hiding place. But you are an intelligent girl, I said so once and I'll say it again. You foisted on me a fairly plausible story. If I had believed it, you would presently have "discovered" the gold, the ransom would have been paid, and all would have been well. You had got rid of Aster, and you and Yen would in due time have evolved another scheme for eloping together and for getting the Min property into your hands.'

A dull rumbling sound came from below. The battering-ram was being rolled over the uneven ground towards the gate of the country house.

Kee-yü fixed the judge with her wide, burning eyes. 'The hungry heart,' he said to himself as he watched her pale, distorted face. Suddenly she burst out:

'You spoiled it all, you dog-official! But I shan't tell you where I hid the gold. So now we shall all die, and you with us!'

'Don't be a fool!' the bailiff shouted at her. He cast a horrified glance over the balustrade at the new group of bandits that came galloping down the slope, brandishing their swords. 'Holy Heaven, you must tell us where the gold is! You can't let me be slaughtered by those beasts! You love me!'

'And therefore you would like to put all the blame on me, eh? Nothing doing, my friend! We shall all die together, go the same way as that little strumpet of yours, your dear Aster!'

'Aster . . . she . . .' Yen stammered. 'What a fool I was not to have stuck to her! She loved me, and asked nothing in return! I didn't want her to be killed, but you, you said

135

she had to go, for our own safety. And I, stupid fool, chose your money and you, you ugly, mean wretch with that large head of yours!' As Kee-yü staggered backwards, the bailiff went on with a choking voice: 'What a splendid woman she was! Think of it, I could have clasped that perfect, pulsating body in my arms, every night! Instead I made love to you, you measly bag of bones, had to join your ineffectual, filthy little games! I hate you, I tell you, I . . .'

An agonized cry sounded behind the judge. He swung round, but he was too late. Kee-yü had thrown herself over the balustrade.

'We are lost!' Yen Yuan shouted. 'Now we can't get the gold! She never told me where . . .'

He broke off, staring down over the balustrade in speechless horror. One of the bandits had jumped from his horse. He walked up to the dead woman lying among the boulders, her head at an unnatural angle. The bandit stooped and tore the rings from her ears. Then he felt in her sleeves. He righted himself, his hands empty. With an angry shout he drew his sword and with one savage, slashing blow cut her belly open.

The bailiff turned round, retching violently. Clasping his hands to his middle he began to vomit. Judge Dee took his arm and pulled him up roughly.

'Speak up!' he snarled. 'Confess how you murdered the woman you loved!'

'I didn't murder her!' the bailiff gasped. 'She said that Aster had seen her when she took the gold, and that she must die. The she-devil had given me a thin blade, she said I would have to do it. But when Kee-yü was facing Aster, and when the poor girl denied having spied on her, she suddenly took the dagger out of my hand. "You liar!" she hissed, pointing the dagger at her breast. "Strip and show me the charms you used to bewitch my man!" After the frightened girl had undressed, she made her stand against

136

'I GRABBED HER AND SHOUTED AT HER TO STOP . . .'

the bed-post, and raise her arms above her head. Aster was shivering in the cold room, but she stiffened in nameless fear as that hideous creature began to touch her breasts and all the rest of her body with the flat of the dagger, making horrible, obscene remarks all the time. Aster moaned in abject terror, every so often she tried to turn away, but the she-devil would let her feel the point of the dagger, and mutter hideous, unspeakable threats at her. And I, I had to stand there helpless, in a deadly fear that in her frenzy she would wound or mutilate the poor, defenceless girl. At last, when Kee-yü let the dagger drop for a moment, I grabbed her shoulders and shouted at her to stop. Kee-yü gave me a contemptuous look. She told the trembling girl haughtily to turn round. Coolly feeling with her left hand for the edge of the shoulder-blade, she plunged the dagger deep into her back.

'I stumbled back, sought support against the wall. Half-stunned, I looked on as she laid Aster on the floor, carefully staunched the bleeding and cleaned the wound, all the time humming a horrible little tune. After she had put a plaster on the wound, she made a neat bundle of Aster's clothes, and dressed her in one of her own white robes. Then she told me to help her lay the dead body on the bed. She tied the girl's sash, as calmly as if she were knotting her own, in front of her dressing-table. It was . . . it was unspeakable, I tell you!'

He buried his face in his hands. When he looked up he asked, making a desperate effort to keep his voice under control:

'How did you find us out?'

'I was set on the right trail by the old landowner's indirect warning, namely his insisting on my staying in his daughter's room. He was fond of her, but he knew how her morbid brooding over her weak health had warped her mind, and he suspected there had been some devilry connected with her death. When I talked to her up in her room, she had herself well under control. But passion is a dangerous thing. One word in praise of Aster, and a few critical remarks about you sufficed to make her betray herself. As to you, Mr Yen, you aren't as good at play-acting as she. The fear of death pervaded this house and all its inmates, except you. You did not, however, impress me as a man of courage. On the contrary, I thought you were a coward—quite correctly, as has now been proved. Yet you spoke in a nearly flippant manner about our impending fate. That was because your thoughts were not on death. They were on life, life in ease and comfort, on your paramour's inherited money. And the elaborate bow of Aster's sash you mentioned just now clinched the case. For only a woman could have tied it in exactly that way. It came so naturally to Kee-yü that it never occurred to her that she was leaving a clue that pointed directly at her.'

The bailiff stared at him, dumbfounded. The judge resumed:

'Well, I believe every word you said just now. Kee-yü was indeed the main criminal, you only her will-less tool. But you are an accomplice to a cruel murder, and therefore you shall be beheaded on the scaffold.'

'Scaffold?' Yen laughed shrilly. His sobbing laughter became mixed with dull thuds from below. 'Listen, you fool! The Flying Tigers are breaking the gate down!'

The judge listened silently. All of a sudden the thuds ceased. It was dead quiet for a brief while. Then there were suddenly loud shouts and curses. The judge leaned over the balustrade.

'Look!' he ordered Yen. 'See how they run!'

The bandits had abandoned the battering-ram. The horsemen were frantically whipping up their horses, while those

139

on foot ran behind them as fast as they could, towards the mountain slope.

'Why . . . why are they running away?' the bewildered bailiff stammered.

The judge turned round and pointed at the river. A large war-junk was being borne swiftly to the shore, the long oars beating the waves in a quick rhythm so as to keep the ship at the right angle for being beached. Coloured banners were fluttering above the long halberds and peaked helmets of the soldiers that crowded the deck. In the stern many caparisoned horses stood tethered close together. Behind the junk came a second one, slightly smaller. Its deck was piled with logs and coils of thick rope. Small men in brown leather jackets and caps were busily mounting wheels to low carts.

'I sent a letter to the commandant of the fortress, last night,' the judge spoke in a level voice. 'I explained that the notorious Flying Tigers were marooned here, and asked for a cavalry force, and a detachment of sappers. While the soldiers are rounding up the bandits, the sappers will repair the bridge over the gap, to enable my escort to get across and join me. In the meantime I shall wind up this murder case here. I expect I shall be able to leave at noon. For I am under orders to proceed to the Imperial capital without undue delay.'

The bailiff stared at the approaching junks with unbelieving eyes.

'How did you get that letter to the fort?' he asked hoarsely.

'I organized flying tigers of my own,' the judge replied curtly. 'I wrote about a dozen identical letters, sealed them and handed them to one of the youngsters whom I had seen flying kites in the afternoon. I told him to attach each copy to a large kite. He was to fly them one after the other. Each time one was high up in the air, he was to cut the string.

With the north wind blowing steadily, I hoped that at least one or two of the brightly-coloured kites would reach the village on the opposite bank, be found and taken to the commandant of the fort. And that is what happened. This is the end of the Flying Tigers, Mr Yen. And your end too.'

POSTSCRIPT

Judge Dee was a historical person. He was born in the fourth year of the Chen-kuan period of the Tang dynasty, i.e. A.D. 630. He died in A.D. 700.

His biography in the Annals of the Tang dynasty states that, during the first half of his long and distinguished official career, when he was serving as district magistrate in the provinces, he solved a great number of difficult criminal cases. Hence he became famous in China as one of the great detectives of former times. He is also celebrated as one of China's great statesmen, for in the second half of his career, after he had been appointed to high office in the capital, he played an important role in the internal and external politics of the Tang Empire. All this is historical fact. The two stories told here, however, are entirely fictitious, and the towns mentioned—Han-yuan, Pei-chow, etc.—have no real existence.

It may be added that astronomy is a very ancient science in China, and that there also it is believed that stellar signs influence the life and destiny of man. The endpapers show a Chinese zodiac, with an explanation of the Chinese sexagenary cycles. There the twelve signs of the zodiac are arranged around the Two Primordial Forces *yin* (negative, female, darkness) and *yang* (positive, male, light) and the Eight Triagrams, *pa-kua*. The halved circle in the centre portrays the eternal interaction of the dual forces *yin* and *yang* (cf. the explanation on p. 59 of my novel *The Haunted Monastery*, published by William Heinemann Ltd, London, 1961). The eight triagrams represent the eight possible combinations of one broken *yin* and one unbroken *yang* line;

these triagrams form the basis of the ancient Book of Divination (cf. *The I Ching or Book of Changes* translated by Richard Wilhelm, with an introduction by C. G. Jung, London, 1950). The dustcover of the present volume is decorated with the same symbolic diagram, with the Chinese characters for 'monkey' and 'tiger' in their archaic forms superimposed and in their correct zodiac positions: west-south-west and east-north-east.

In Chinese astrology a person's character and career are analysed on the basis of the cyclical signs under which he is born, and formerly no betrothal was concluded until a comparative study of the cyclical signs of the year, date and hour of birth of either partner had proved the couple to be well matched.

Judge Dee was born in A.D. 630, i.e. the year VII-3, a year of the Tiger, belonging to the element *metal*, and influenced by the planet Venus. The date and hour of his birth have not been recorded.

As to the seven-stringed lute (in form resembling a psaltery) that is mentioned in the second story, it should be noted that the Chinese consider its music the highest expression of classical, purely Chinese musical art; it produces a quiet, refined music, entirely different from, for instance, later Chinese theatre music, which was greatly influenced by the music from Central Asia. In China good antique lutes, *ku-ch'in*, are prized as highly as a Stradivarius violin with us, and there also the secret of the superior tone rests on the quality of the varnish covering the sound-box. Connoisseurs judge the age of an antique lute by the shape of the tiny bursts that in course of time appear on the lacquered surface. Readers interested in this fascinating subject may be referred to my book *The Lore of the Chinese Lute*, Monumenta Nipponica Monographs, Sophia University, Tokyo, 1940.

ROBERT VAN GULIK